John M. F. Ludlow

President Lincoln

self-pourtrayed

John M. F. Ludlow

President Lincoln
self-pourtrayed

ISBN/EAN: 9783337276805

Printed in Europe, USA, Canada, Australia, Japan

Cover: Foto ©Raphael Reischuk / pixelio.de

More available books at **www.hansebooks.com**

PRESIDENT LINCOLN

SELF-POURTRAYED.

BY

JOHN MALCOLM LUDLOW.

Published for the benefit of the British and Foreign
Freedmen's Aid Society.

LONDON:

ALFRED W. BENNETT, 5, BISHOPSGATE WITHOUT:

ALEXANDER STRAHAN, 148, STRAND;

HAMILTON, ADAMS & Co., 33, PATERNOSTER ROW.

1866.

CONTENTS.

NOTE.

THIS volume represents (with a few trifling alterations and some additions) the uncurtailed text of three papers written for " Good Words," under the title of "President Lincoln Judged by his own Words," but which, through the exigencies of periodical publication, had to be compressed into two (August and December, 1865.)

The main source from which the original papers were derived, was Mr. Raymond's earlier work, the " History of the Administration of President Lincoln" (New York, 1864), now superseded by his " Life and Public Services of Abraham Lincoln." From this latter volume I have borrowed, with but few exceptions, the additions now introduced. An earlier article by myself, also published in " Good Words," has also been appended.

I need hardly say that the work in no sense pretends to be a biography of the late President, the greater part of whose life is known as yet only in outline to the public.

J. M. L.

PRESIDENT LINCOLN

SELF-POURTRAYED.

"By thy words thou shalt be justified, and by thy words thou shalt be condemned."

CHAPTER I.

To the Beginning of the War, April 14-15, 1861.

The year of our Lord 1865 will leave its mark upon the record of the ages. It has witnessed the close of the most gigantic, the most unparalleled among civil wars. And, as almost the last scene in that great Transatlantic tragedy, it has witnessed an event which, of itself, would have sufficed to stamp such a mark for all time;—the murder, in the midst of his own people, of the twice-chosen ruler of the greatest of earth's republics. Before the purely human emotions excited by that event have entirely died away from our memories—from our hearts—it is well, I think, to consider whether the sudden halo of universal regret which flashed into being round the memory of the late President of the United States, on the news of his assassination, sprang only from those emotions, and is to pass away like them, or whether.it is really the abiding glory of a noble and righteous life. With this view I should like to judge Abraham Lincoln out of his own mouth, by his own recorded words; selecting, moreover, for the purpose, almost exclusively those belonging to the period of his presidency,—words which, in fact, under the fires of that terrific crisis which seems only now coming to an end, must have had all the weight and metal of very deeds, if they were not to burn up the utterer himself. Even of these I shall have space but to notice a few; referring my readers for an ampler collection of them to Mr. H. J. Raymond's " Life and

Public Services of Abraham Lincoln " (New York, 1865).

Of Mr. Lincoln's life itself, prior to his election as President, the briefest sketch must here suffice.* Born 12th of February, 1809, of a poor white family in the slave State of Kentucky—and Mr. Beecher has said that he knows " nothing lower than that"—he had at least the blessing of a Christian mother, and of a father who, though uneducated himself, sent his child to school, and migrated from slave into free soil, literally hewing his way for the last few miles to his future home. After earning his

---

* Not so brief, however, as his own, sent, in 1858, to the compiler of the "Dictionary of Congress :"—

" Born February 12th, 1809, in Harden County, Kentucky.

Education defective.

Profession, a lawyer.

Have been a Captain of Volunteers in Black Hawk war.

Postmaster of a very small office.

Four times a Member of the Illinois Legislature, and was a Member of the Lower House of Congress."

livelihood first by manual labour, then (after a
bit of soldiering in 1832,* and an unsuccessful
venture as a store-keeper), like George Washington before him, by surveying, Abraham Lincoln entered the legislature of his adoptive State,
Illinois, in 1834, began thereupon the study of
law, received his "license" in 1836, and prac-

---

* Thus humorously described by himself, in after life,
while in Congress :—

"By the way, Mr. Speaker, did you know I was a
military hero ? Yes, sir, in the days of the Black Hawk
war I fought, bled, and came away. Speaking of General
Cass's career reminds me of my own. I was not at
Sullivan's defeat, but I was about as near to it as Cass
was to Hull's surrender, and, like him, I saw the place
soon after. It is quite certain that I did not break my
sword, for I had none to break ; but I bent my musket
pretty badly on one occasion. If Cass broke his sword,
the idea is, he broke it in desperation. I bent the
musket by accident. If General Cass went in advance
of me in picking whortleberries, I guess I surpassed
him in charges upon the wild onions. If he saw any
live fighting Indians, it was more than I did ; but I had
a great many bloody struggles with the mosquitoes ; and,
although I never fainted from loss of blood, I certainly
can say I was often very hungry."

tised the law as a profession from 1837 to the time of his election to the Presidency. During this period of twenty-four years, besides sitting occasionally in the State Legislature, he was elected in 1847 to the House of Representatives of the United States, where he signalised himself by a motion, by way of amendment, for declaring free, after January 1, 1850 (but with compensation to the owners), all slaves born within the district of Columbia (that small space of fifty square miles, carved out of slave-soil, which, by a peculiar provision of the United States Constitution, is under the immediate government of Congress); was twice a candidate for the United States' Senate; and stood, in 1856, second on the list of Republican candidates for the Vice-Presidency of the United States. Roughly speaking, his life thus divides itself into two nearly equal portions, the latter of which was spent in the practice of the law. The fact is only worth pointing out by way of rebuke to the puppyism of such would-be gentlemen as, in the barrister-attorney of nearly twenty-five years' standing, who, on the 4th of

March, 1861, ascended the steps of the Capitol of Washington as first magistrate of the United States, long refused to see anything else but a " rail-splitter" or a " bargee."

It was the lot of Abraham Lincoln to embody in his own person the first signal triumph of the principles which he professed. Up to the time of his election, the United States were ruled by the slave-owners of the South, allied to the so-called " Democrats" of the North. He was, moreover, citizen of a State (Illinois) which, although free, bordered to the south and partly to the west on two slave States, Kentucky and Missouri, and was as hostile to the slave himself as to his chains (since her " Black Laws," forbidding the sojourn of coloured people upon her soil, &c., have only been repealed within the last few months), and various of whose most prominent citizens were themselves slave-owners beyond her borders. It was under these circumstances that Abraham Lincoln fought his way into public notice as an anti-slavery politician.

The most insidious form in which the slavery

question was at this time presented to the people, was that of the doctrine of "squatter sovereignty," as it was termed,—viz., that of the absolute right of emigrants (white emigrants, be it understood) into United States territory not yet organised into States, to introduce or forbid slavery at pleasure ; thus contravening not only the known purpose of the chief founders of the Republic, that slavery, whilst suffered to exist where it was already, should not be allowed to extend its limits,* but the later compromise with the slave-holding interest, known as the " Missouri Compromise," which expressly prohibited slavery beyond a given parallel of latitude. Of this doctrine of " squatter sovereignty," Mr. Douglas, the "little giant" of Illinois, was the most prominent expounder, and it was generally favoured by the Democratic party at the North. Mr. Lincoln, in the

---

* It should never be forgotten that a proposal to this effect, put forward in 1784 by the Virginian slave-owner, Jefferson, only failed to become law by the accidental absence of a New Jersey delegate.

course of his first popular contest with Mr. Douglas, in 1854, when the question was that of its applicability to the territories of Kansas and Nebraska, situate in great measure north of the Missouri Compromise line, and from which, according to the terms of that compromise, slavery should so far have been distinctly excluded, met the doctrine with sturdy good sense. "I admit," he said, "that the emigrant to Kansas and Nebraska is competent to govern himself; but I deny his right to govern any other person without that person's consent." But the same question was again at issue in Mr. Lincoln's second contest for the senatorship with Mr. Douglas, in 1858 ; and again the former took up the broad ground of opposition to slavery in principle. "Slavery is wrong," he said, in a speech at Cincinnati, in the free State of Ohio, but in the immediate neighbourhood of the slave State of Kentucky, and to a mixed audience from both States. He was hissed for the words, and continued :—

"I acknowledge that you must maintain your

opposition just there, if at all. But I find that
every man comes into the world with a mouth
to be fed and a back to be clothed; that each
has also two hands; and I infer that those hands
were meant to feed that mouth and to clothe
that back. And I warn you, Kentuckians, that
whatever institution would fetter those hands
from so doing, violates that justice which is
the only political wisdom, and is sure to tumble
around those who seek to uphold it. ". . .
Your hisses will not blow down the walls of
justice. Slavery is wrong; the denial of that
truth has brought on the angry conflict of
brother with brother; it has kindled the fires
of civil war in houses; it has raised the portents
that overhang the future of our nation. And
be you sure that no compromise, no political
arrangement with slavery, will ever last, which
does not deal with it as a great wrong."

The above prophetic passage, which the
timidity of Mr. Lincoln's party suppressed in
the printed records of his speech, was noted
down at the time by one who was latterly a

political opponent of Mr. Lincoln (Mr. M. D. Conway, who has since reproduced it in the " Fortnightly Review "). But it is not more prophetic than were the opening words of Mr. Lincoln's previous speech to the convention which had nominated him :—

" A house divided against itself cannot stand. I believe this government cannot endure permanently half-slave and half-free. I do not expect the Union to be dissolved—I do not expect the house to fall ; but I do expect it will cease to be divided. It will become all one thing or all the other."

Side by side, however, with passages like the above, which fully prefigure the grander aspects of Mr. Lincoln's career, we must not overlook the indications of an influence which gave to it also occasionally an aspect of hesitancy, and of at least momentary littleness. In the latter half of the history of the United States, prior to the Secession outbreak, one of the most prominent names is that of Henry Clay. A name not to be looked for in the list of American

Presidents; for it is a singularity of that history that, after the passing through office of Washington and his great contemporaries, the foremost men—Jackson excepted—do not fill the foremost place, but, standing a little behind in official rank, quite overshadow the actual Presidents. During this period, three such men typify three different modes of feeling: Daniel Webster, of Massachusetts, the hard Northern feeling, opposed to slavery, caring little for the slave, but devotedly attached to the Union, and scarcely less so to the commercial interests of the North;—John C. Calhoun, of South Carolina, the hard and haughty Southern feeling, caring little for the Union, but devoted to Southern supremacy and to slavery, not in itself, but as the main pivot of that supremacy;—Henry Clay, of Kentucky, finally, the temper of the Border Slave States, capable from its position of sympathising with both parties, anxious to unite both, convinced of the wrong and mischief of slavery, and yet crushed beneath a sense of the difficulty of med-

dling with it, and thereby driven into perpetual
contradictions between principles and practice,
and to the scheming of endless compromises
between the fierce opposing interests on both
sides.   To the distant observer, this last type of
character will generally be the least attractive
of the three.   Each of the others seems to have
a unity of purpose which it wants; it seems un-
stable, shifty, always occupied with small details.
But Clay's unswerving faithfulness to the Union,
and his never retracted, never qualified con-
demnation of slavery, together with the purity
of his personal character, and his unquestioned
abilities as a statesman and an orator, gave him
a singularly high place in the estimation of his
countrymen.   His " Life " had been one of the
first books placed in the hands of his young
brother-Kentuckian, and in the course of the
contest with Douglas we find him speaking of
Henry Clay as " my *beau-ideal* of a statesman—
the man for whom I fought all my humble life."
In this choice of a political hero in one who,
though opposed utterly to slavery in principle,

yet spent his life in the vain effort to effect compromises between it and freedom, will be found,
I think, the explanation of much in Abraham
Lincoln's Presidential conduct which has been
harshly judged by the out-and-out Abolitionist.

Till 1860, however, as we have seen, Abraham
Lincoln is mainly known by his defeats. Yet
the man knows his worth. He has sat in the
great council of his nation, though only in its
really *lower* house. But he has deemed himself
fit for the higher,—for that Senate which has
always been the goal of honourable ambition in
the United States,—nay, for the Speakership
of that Senate itself, which belongs to the Vice-
President, the second officer in the State. The
day comes when he is put forward for the very
highest office, and he does not shrink from the
contest. If the people prefer him to the greatest
orator of the day, to the very leader of the Republican party hitherto, Mr. Seward, the Illinois
lawyer will accept their confidence. But he
remains in his own town of Springfield, whilst
the Republican Convention of 465 delegates is

meeting at Chicago.   As he sits in a news-
paper office (May 18, 1860), speaking with some
friends, a message comes from the Superinten-
dent of the Telegraph Company:—"Mr. Lincoln, you are nominated on the third ballot."
His first words are the simplest, homeliest, that
could have fallen from human lips:—"There's a
little woman down at our house would like to hear
this—I'll go down and tell her."   With those
sweet words of a husband's holy love, Abraham
Lincoln entered upon that career, which in less
than five years was to end in a martyr's death.
Was ever the highest power received in a gentler
spirit ?

On the next day his nomination was formally
announced to him, together with the resolutions
adopted by the Convention, forming what was
termed the "Chicago Platform," the main
feature of which was a pledge against the extension of slavery to the Territories.   After four
days' consideration, he accepted both (23rd
May) by letter, concluding in words chiefly remarkable for the entire freedom from partizan

spirit which they show in this candidate of a party :—

"Imploring the assistance of Divine Providence, and with due regard to the views and feelings of all who were represented in the Convention, to the rights of all the States, and Territories, and people of the nation, to the inviolability of the Constitution, and the perpetual union, harmony, and prosperity of all, I am most happy to co-operate for the practical success of the principles declared by the Convention."

The nomination was a successful one. On the 6th November, 1860, Mr. Lincoln was elected President of the United States by the unanimous vote of all the free States, except New Jersey, which gave him four votes out of her seven, making 180 votes in the "Electoral College," which names the Presidents; the votes cast for all three opposing candidates summing up only 123. Of the popular vote, however, which names the Electoral College, Mr. Lincoln had not obtained an absolute majority, but 1,857,610, against 2,804,560 given to his opponents ; yet out of this latter number all but 847,953 were cast in favour of candidates professedly supporting the Union. In other words, out of 4,662,170 voters, 3,814,217, or more than three-fourths, were in favour of the Union as a paramount principle ; 1,857,610, or nearly two-fifths, were in favour of the Union, and of rigidly restricting slavery from further extension ; and 547,953, or not a fifth, for slavery as a paramount principle ; but these few wielded the whole mass of the slave country, except the border States of Kentucky, Virginia, Missouri, and Tennessee, the eastern part of which last has long been practically almost free soil. In these figures lies indeed the whole history of the Secession war.

Abraham Lincoln was now President of the United States. By a curious provision of their Constitution, he was not yet to enter upon the functions of his office. His predecessor, Mr. Buchanan, who had not even been nominated as a candidate, had for four months yet to retain the Presidency in his imbecile hands. During that period, ordinances of secession were passed by Conventions in no less than seven States (South Carolina, 20th December, 1860; Mississippi, January 9, 1861; Florida, January 10; Alabama, January 11; Georgia, January 19; Louisiana, January 26; Texas, February 5). Delegates from the seceding States had met in another convention at Montgomery in Alabama (February 4), had adopted a provisional constitution, appointed and inaugurated (February 18) a President and a Vice-President; and the former, Mr. Jefferson Davis, in an address delivered on his arrival at Montgomery, had declared that "the time for compromise has now passed, and the South is determined to maintain her position, and make all who oppose her smell Southern powder and feel Southern steel, if coercion is persisted in." Meanwhile, Mr. Buchanan was advised by his Attorney-General that Congress had no right to carry on war against any State, and remained quiescent accordingly, even while forts, arsenals, and other Government property were being seized on all

c

sides by the seceding States: although by the
8th January he had got so far as to declare that
it was his right and his duty "to use military
force defensively against those who resist the
Federal officers in the execution of their legal
functions, and against those who assail the property of the Federal Government." Congress,
on its side, notwithstanding the withdrawal of
most of the senators and representatives from
the seceding States, had made almost every con-
ceivable concession to the South, adopting in
principle an amendment to the Constitution
which should forbid for ever any intermeddling
by Federal action with slavery in any State;
conceding "squatter sovereignty" so far as to
create governments for three new territories
without forbiddance of slavery; severely censur-
ing those free States which had passed laws to
hinder the recovery of fugitive slaves.

During all this time, till the 11th February,
1861, the new President remained absolutely
silent. Not a word fell from him which could hinder Mr. Buchanan from saving the Union in his

own way. On the 11th February Mr. Lincoln opened his lips anew as he left his home; and during his slow progress to Washington, which he reached on the 23rd, not a day passed but what his voice was heard in replies to the addresses of his countrymen. His first words on this triumphal progress to his eventual martyrdom, being his farewell to his fellow-townsmen at Springfield, must be quoted at length :—

" My friends,—No one not in my position can appreciate the sadness I feel at this parting. To this people I owe all that I am. Here I have lived more than a quarter of a century ; here my children were born, and here one of them lies buried. I know not how soon I shall see you again. A duty devolves upon me which is perhaps greater than that which has devolved upon any other man since the days of Washington. He never would have succeeded except for the aid of Divine Providence, upon which he at all times relied. I feel that I cannot succeed without the same Divine aid which sustained him, and on the same Almighty Being I place

c 2

my reliance for support; and I hope you, my friends, will all pray that I may receive that Divine assistance without which I cannot succeed, but with which success is certain. Again I bid you all an affectionate farewell."

Weighty and touching words, surely. The momentary pleasure which he had felt on finding himself chosen as candidate for the highest office in the State by a large body of his fellow-countrymen, and which he could not enjoy without sharing it with the "little woman" at home, has quite vanished away into the sorrow of parting with the quiet memories of so many years of private life, into the awe of the dark future. Not a shot has yet been fired; but he knows that a duty has devolved upon him, greater perhaps than has devolved upon any since Washington. Yet he sinks not crushed beneath that duty, but strengthens himself against it like a man, looking up through the darkness to that Hand which sustained Washington, and which he trusts to sustain himself. And as he thus departs to rule over the many millions of his people, he asks his friends and his neighbours for their prayers. (And clever people in Europe, meanwhile, were saying and writing that God is an idea, and that Christ was an impostor, and that the Christian faith is a delusion ; and Mr. Carlyle was trying to puff into a hero, for the special admiration of the nineteenth century, that cross between fox and wolf, Frederic II. of Prussia.) Surely, from that hour, the day of shams had for America passed away; the true, honest man had gone forth in the fear of God, conquering and to conquer.

It were idle to attempt recording here all Mr. Lincoln's speeches on this journey to Washington. Without entering into any controversy, into any single detail of policy which could hamper the government, you see him appealing earnestly to the broad principles of patriotism, stirring up, yet without any bitterness, the energies of his countrymen on behalf of the Union. He warns them that it is for them, not for him, to save the country:—

"In all trying positions in which I shall be placed, and doubtless I shall be placed in many such, my reliance will be placed upon you and the people of the United States. I wish you to remember, now and for ever, that it is your business, and not mine; that if the union of these States, and the liberties of this people shall be lost, it is but little to any one man of fifty-two years of age, but a great deal to the thirty millions of people who inhabit these United States, and to their posterity in all coming time. It is your business to rise up and preserve the Union and liberty for yourselves, and not for me. I, as already intimated, am but an accidental instrument, temporary, and to serve but for a limited time; and I appeal to you again to constantly bear in mind that with you, and not with politicians, not with Presidents, not with office-seekers, but with you, is the question:—'Shall the Union, and shall the liberties of this country be preserved to the latest generations?'"—*Speech at Indianopolis, Feb.* 11.

He insists on his own insignificance :—

" I cannot but know what you all know, that without a name, perhaps without a reason why I should have a name, there has fallen upon me a task such as did not rest even upon the Father of his Country ; and so feeling, I cannot but turn and look for the support without which it will be impossible for me to perform that great task. I turn, then, and look to the great American people, and to that God who has never forsaken them."—*Speech at Columbus, Ohio, Feb.* 13.

He appeals to his political opponents for support :—

" I understand myself to be received here by the representatives of the people of New Jersey, a majority of whom differ in opinion from those with whom I have acted. This manifestation is therefore to be regarded by me as expressing their devotion to the Union, the Constitution, and the liberties of the people. I shall do all that may be in my power to promote a peaceful settlement of all our difficulties. The man does not live who is more devoted to peace than I am.

None who would do more to preserve it: but it may be necessary to put the foot down firmly. And if I do my duty, and do right, you will sustain me, will you not? Received as I am by the members of a legislature, the majority of whom do not agree with me in political sentiments, I trust that I may have their assistance in piloting the ship of State through this voyage, surrounded by perils as it is; for if it should suffer wreck now, there will be no pilot ever needed for another voyage."—*Speech at Trenton, New Jersey, Feb. 21.*

He asserts his unchangeable faith in the principles of that famous Declaration of American Independence, which declared all men to be " created equal," and endowed by their Creator with the " inalienable rights " of "life, liberty, and the pursuit of happiness ":—

" I have never had a feeling, politically, that did not spring from the sentiments embodied in the Declaration of Independence. I have often pondered over the dangers which were incurred by the men who assembled here, and framed and

adopted that Declaration of Independence. I
have pondered over the toils that were endured
by the officers and soldiers of the army who
achieved that Independence. I have often in-
quired of myself what great principle or idea it
was that.kept this Confederacy so long together.
It was not the mere matter of the separation of
the colonies from the mother land, but that
sentiment in the Declaration of Independence
which gave liberty, not alone to the people of
this country, but, I hope, to the world, for all
future time. It was that which gave promise
that in due time the weight should be lifted
from the shoulders of all men. . . . Now, my
friends, can this country be saved upon that
basis? If it can, I will consider myself one of
the happiest men in the world if I can help to
save it. . . . But if this country cannot be
saved without giving up that principle, I was
about to say *I would rather be assassinated on this
spot than surrender it.*"—*Speech at Philadelphia in
' Independence Hall,' Feb.* 21.

The effort successfully made by Mr. Lincoln,

during all this series of speeches, to preserve silence as to all questions of detail, must have been a violent one; for no stag at bay amidst the unleashed hounds could be more beset than he was by throngs of anxious questioners, whilst he himself must have been often sorely tempted to speak out.

He said at New York (February 19):—

"I have been in the habit of thinking and speaking sometimes upon political questions that have for some years past agitated the country; and if I were disposed to do so, and we could take up some one of the issues, as the lawyers call them, and I were called upon to make an argument about it to the best of my ability, I could do it without much preparation. . . . . I have not kept silence since the Presidential election from any party wantonness, or from any indifference to the anxiety that pervades the minds of men about the aspect of the political affairs of their country. . . . . I do suppose that, while the political drama being enacted in this country at this time is rapidly

shifting its scenes . . . . it was peculiarly fitting
that I should see it all, up to the last minute,
before I should take ground, that I might be
disposed, by the shifting of the scenes afterwards, also to shift. I have said several times
upon this journey, and I now repeat it to you,
that when the time does come, I shall then take
the ground that I think is right—right for the
North, for the South, for the East, for the West,
for the whole country."

But while thus acting in obedience to the
promptings of his own sense of duty, we now
see that Mr. Lincoln was in fact doing precisely
that which was best for his country, displaying
the most practical and consummate wisdom.
By his every speech, at every stage of his journey, he was lifting men above the sphere of
party politics and personal preferences into that
of political duty, and of the broadest statesmanship; compelling them to forget himself, his
predecessor yet in office, his late competitors, in
the one great question, "How shall our country
be saved?" And thus—tearing away as it were

by armfuls at every step the thick undergrowth of selfishness and mutual prejudice, which was at once choking the good qualities of the American people, and obscuring the massive foundations of the American polity, its pledges of equal right, and freedom, and justice, through mutual help, to all,—he hewed his way, so to speak, like a true backwoodsman, to the national capital at Washington, and to that "White House" or Presidential mansion, from which his murdered body was one day to issue forth amidst the sorrow of the civilized world.* Here indeed the series of his unofficial speeches closes (Feb. 28), with expressions of the friendliest nature towards the South :—

" I have reached this city of Washington under circumstances considerably differing from those under which any other man has ever reached it. I am here for the purpose of taking an official

---

* It should not be forgotten that there was a plot to murder him on his way through Baltimore to Washington, to take up his Presidential duties, which he baffled by taking an earlier train than the one fixed on.

position among the people, almost all of whom were politically opposed to me, and are yet opposed, as I suppose. . . . . Much of the ill feeling that has existed between you and the people of your surroundings, and that people from among whom I came, has depended, and now depends, upon a misunderstanding. I hope that I may have it in my power to remove something of this misunderstanding, that I may be enabled to convince you, and the people of your section of the country, that we regard you as in all things our equals, and in all things entitled to the same respect and the same treatment that we claim for ourselves; that we are in nowise disposed, if it were in our power, to oppress you, to deprive you of any of your rights under the Constitution of the United States, or even narrowly to split hairs with you in regard to those rights, but are determined to give you, as far as lies in our hands, all your rights under the Constitution—not grudgingly, but fully and fairly. I hope that, by thus dealing with you, we will become better acquainted and better friends."

In the first of his state papers, his "Inaugural Address" (March 4, 1861), Mr. Lincoln begins by disclaiming the purpose and the right "to interfere with slavery in the States where it exists." He admits the constitutional obligation of rendering up fugitive slaves; but he asks whether, in any law upon the giving up of slaves, "all the safeguards of liberty known in civilized and humane jurisprudence" ought not to be introduced, "so that a free man be not in any case surrendered as a slave?" And with an implied censure of that absolute denial of United States' citizenship to the coloured man, which had been shamefully practised of late years, he asks equally, whether it might not be well "to provide by law for the enforcement of that clause in the Constitution which guarantees that the citizens of each state shall be entitled to all privileges and immunities of citizens in the several States?" The slave-power, in other words, shall have its pound of flesh, but not a drop of blood besides. Whatever legal privileges stand written to its credit, let it enjoy; but the spirit of slavery shall not penetrate into the law itself. The fugitive shall be presumed free until proved a slave ; the coloured citizen of free Massachusetts or free New York, shall stand on the same legal footing as the white citizen in slave Georgia or slave Mississippi. But it is the preservation of the Union, of the national life, which above all engrosses him, since disruption is now "formidably attempted :"

" I hold that in contemplation of universal law, and of the Constitution, the union of these States is perpetual. Perpetuity is implied, if not expressed, in the fundamental law of all national governments. It is safe to assert that no government proper ever had a provision in its organic law for its own termination. . . . No State, upon its own mere motion, can lawfully get out of the Union. . . . I therefore consider that, in view of the Constitution and the laws, the Union is unbroken ; and to the extent of my ability I shall take care, as the Constitution itself expressly enjoins upon me, that the laws of the Union be faithfully executed in all the States. Doing this I deem to be only a simple duty on my part, and I shall perform it so far as practicable, unless my rightful masters, the American people, shall withhold the requisite means, or in some authoritative manner direct the contrary. I trust this will not be regarded as a menace, but only as the declared purpose of the Union, that it will constitutionally defend and maintain itself. In doing this there need be no bloodshed or violence; and there shall be none, unless it be forced upon the national authority. The power confided to me will be used to hold, occupy, and possess the property and places belonging to the Government, and to collect the duties and imposts; but beyond what may be but necessary for these objects, there will be no invasion, no using of force against or among the people anywhere. Where hostility to the United States in any interior locality shall be so great and universal as to prevent competent resident citizens from holding the Federal offices, there will be no attempt to force obnoxious strangers among the people for that object. . .

So far as possible, the people everywhere shall have that sense of perfect security which is most favourable to calm thought and reflection. The course here indicated will be followed, unless current events and experience shall show a modification or change to be proper; and in every case and exigency my best discretion will be exercised, according to circumstances actually existing, and with a view and a hope of a peaceful solution of the national troubles, and the restoration of fraternal sympathies and affections."

Let us pause for an instant over this passage; for it indicates, at the outset, a remarkable feature of Abraham Lincoln's mind,—a very fallible appreciation of the immediate consequences of events, coupled with an abiding sense that the future must always be larger than what he sees of it, and that therefore he must not pledge himself irrevocably to any future course of action, even that which seems to him for the time the wisest and fairest. We all know how utterly his hope of "a peaceful solution of the national

D

troubles" went to wreck. We all know how unprofitable to the South was the season afforded to
it of "calm thought and reflection." We all
know how soon the Government had to use force
for other purposes than that of holding, occupying, and possessing the property and places
belonging to it—had to invade State after State,
and to force "obnoxious strangers" among the
people of each. But an unerring instinct had
guarded Abraham Lincoln from mistaking on any
of these points his own notions for the realities
of things. He had from the first taken into
account the possibility of those modifications
and changes which "current events and experience" might show to be proper. He had
reserved his "best discretion" for every case and
exigency. And thus he went forth to his work
free-handed, unfettered by those pledges of self-
conceit which can manacle down a giant to a
dwarf's weakness.

He now proceeds to plead with those who
really love the Union. Has "any right plainly
written in the Constitution" been denied? He

thinks not. "All our Constitutional contro-
versies" have sprung from the absence of express provisions in the Constitution. "Shall
fugitives from labour be surrendered by national or by State authority? The Constitution
does not expressly say. May Congress prohibit
slavery in the Territories? The Constitution
does not expressly say. Must Congress protect
slavery in the Territories? The Constitution
does not expressly say."

"Upon such questions we divide into ma-
jorities and minorities. If the minority does
not acquiesce, the majority must, or the Government must cease. . . . If a minority,
in such case, will secede rather than acquiesce,
they make a precedent which, in time, will
divide and ruin them; for a minority of their
own will secede from them whenever a majority
refuses to be controlled by such minority. For
instance, why may not any portion of a new
Confederacy, a year or two hence, arbitrarily
secede again, precisely as portions of the present
Union now claim to secede from it? . . .

D 2

Plainly, the central idea of secession is the essence of anarchy. A majority held in restraint by constitutional checks and limitations, and always changing easily with deliberate changes of popular opinions and sentiments, is the only true sovereign of a free people. Whoever rejects it, does of necessity fly to anarchy or to despotism. Unanimity is impossible ; the rule of a minority, as a permanent arrangement, is wholly inadmissible. . . . One section of our country believes that slavery is right, and ought to be extended ; while the other believes it is wrong, and ought not to be extended. This is the only substantial dispute. The fugitive slave clause of the Constitution, and the law for the suppression of the foreign slave-trade, are each as well enforced, perhaps, as any law can ever be in a community where the moral sense of the people imperfectly supports the law itself. The great body of the people abide by the dry legal obligation in both cases, and a few break over in each. This, I think, cannot be perfectly cured ; and it would be worse in both cases after the separation of the sections than before. The foreign slave-trade, now imperfectly suppressed, would be ultimately revived without restrictions in one section; while fugitive slaves, now only partially surrendered, would not be surrendered at all by the other. Physically speaking, we cannot separate. We cannot remove our respective sections from each other, nor build an impassable wall between them. A husband and wife may be divorced, and go out of the presence and beyond the reach of each other; but the different parts of our country cannot do this. They cannot but remain face to face; and intercourse, either amicable or hostile, must continue between them. It is impossible, then, to make that intercourse more advantageous, or more satisfactory, after separation than before. Can aliens make treaties easier than friends can make laws? Can treaties be more faithfully enforced between aliens than laws can among friends? . . . The chief magistrate derives all his authority from the people, and they have conferred none upon him to fix terms for the separation of the States. . . . His duty is to administer the present government as it came to his hands, and to transmit it, unimpaired by him, to his successor. Why should there not be a patient confidence in the ultimate justice of the people? Is there any better or equal hope in the world? In our present differences is either party without faith of being in the right? If the Almighty Ruler of nations, with His eternal truth and justice, be on your side of the North, or on yours of the South, that truth and that justice will surely prevail, by the judgment of this great tribunal of the American people. By the frame of the government under which we live, the same people have wisely given their public servants but little power for mischief, and have with equal wisdom provided for the return of that little to their own hands at very short intervals. While the people retain their virtue and vigilance, no administration, by any extreme of wickedness or folly, can very seriously injure the Government in the short space of four years. My countrymen, one and all, think calmly and well upon this whole subject.

Nothing valuable can be lost by taking time. If there be an object to hurry any of you in hot haste to a step which you would never take deliberately, that object will be frustrated by taking time; but no good object can be frustrated by it. . . . In your hands, my dissatisfied fellow-countrymen, and not in mine, is the momentous issue of civil war. The Government will not assail you. You can have no conflict without being yourselves the aggressors. You have no oath registered in heaven to destroy the Government; while I have the most solemn one to ' preserve, protect, and defend it.' I am loth to close. We are not enemies, but friends. We must not be enemies. Though passion may have strained, it must not break our bonds of affection. The mystic cords of memory, stretching from every battle-field and patriot grave to every living heart and hearth-stone all over this broad land, will yet swell the chorus of the Union, when again touched, as surely they will be, by the better angels of our nature."

To the President's appeals in favour of con-

cord, or at least calm deliberation, the South
replied (April 12) by the bombardment of Fort
Sumter in Charleston Harbour, which was evacuated on the 14th (others say the 15th). The
President now issued (April 15) a proclamation,
by which, after stating that "the laws of United
States" had been for some time past and were
then "opposed and the execution thereof ob-
structed in the States of South Carolina, Georgia,
Alabama, Florida, Mississippi, and Texas, by
combinations too powerful to be suppressed by
the ordinary course of judicial proceedings, or
by the powers vested in the marshals by law,'
in virtue of the power vested in him by the
Constitution and the laws, he called forth "the
militia of the several States of the Union, to
the aggregate number of 75,000, in order to
suppress said combinations, and to cause the
laws to be duly executed." Appealing "to all
loyal citizens to favour, facilitate, and aid this
effort to maintain the honour, the integrity,
and existence of our national Union, and the
perpetuity of popular government, and to

redress wrongs already long enough endured,"
he stated "that the first service assigned to the
forces hereby called forth, will probably be to
repossess the forts, places, and property which
have been seized from the Union ; and in every
event the utmost care will be observed, consistently with the objects aforesaid, to avoid
any devastation, any destruction of or interference with property, or any disturbance of
peaceful citizens of any part of the country ; "
commanded the persons composing the combinations aforesaid to disperse and retire peaceably to their respective abodes within twenty
days; and, finally, convened both Houses of
Congress for the 4th of July.

Not a day, it will be seen, had been lost. No
lengthened deliberations had been required.
Abraham Lincoln had fulfilled the pledge that
he had repeatedly given on his journey to Washington,—that, when the time did come, he
would take the ground which he thought was
right. He *had* taken it at once, now that the
time was come. And that ground was—law,

and the need of enforcing it. It is this which
gives so grandly conservative a character to the
late war on the Federal side. It has been
simply an effort to suppress combinations against
the law. The tipstaff, or at best the policeman,
ought to have been sufficient for the purpose; it
is only because they are not that the President
now calls out 75,000 militiamen, and will call
into the field army after army, until at last
enough has been done " to suppress said combinations, and to cause the laws to be duly
executed." From this deep abiding sense of
the lawfulness of his position, flows that studi-
ous moderation, that seemingly impassive dry-
ness of tone, which marks all Mr. Lincoln's state
papers, as compared with the subtle yet tumid
rhetoric, the heated appeals to the feelings and
passions of the South, which characterise those
of Mr. Davis. Mr. Lincoln is simply fulfilling
a duty himself, in calling upon others to fulfil
theirs. *That* bears no rhetoric ; *that* appeals
to no passion.

Observe again for the second time the prescient caution which qualifies the pledge to avoid devastation, destruction, or interference with property. The day is not very far off when it may become impossible, consistently with the object of suppressing " said combinations," and causing " the laws to be duly executed," not to interfere with, not to impair, not, finally, to destroy the most precious property in the South, that in human flesh. But in doing this, as well as in sanctioning (how reluctantly always is well known) other acts of devastation and destruction which military expediency may seem to command, the President will violate no pledge, he will but yield to what he deems a necessity. If thus only and not otherwise can illegal combinations be put down, and the execution of the laws be restored, he will be but carrying out by different means the object of this his first proclamation.

The great American civil war, then, has begun. The South has flung down the gauntlet; the North, by its chosen President, has taken it up.

CHAPTER II.

From the Opening of the Civil War to the Emancipation Proclamation of January 1, 1863.

WHEN Congress met in Extraordinary Session on July 4, 1861, four more States had seceded—Virginia (April 25), Arkansas (May 6), North Carolina (May 20), and Tennessee (June 8); the secession being, however, if I am not mistaken, in no single instance submitted to the vote of the people, whilst the Governors of the Border States of Kentucky and Missouri were attempting to take up a position of neutrality, and Secession movements in Maryland had had to be suppressed, chiefly through the somewhat high-handed energy of General Butler. The Confederate capital had been established at Richmond, as if to bid defiance by its proximity to Washington. General Lee — the

favourite Aide-de-Camp of the old Federal
Commander-in-Chief, General Scott—had been
appointed to the chief command of the military
and naval forces of Virginia. The National
Armoury at Harper's Ferry and the Navy
Yard at Gosport had been burned to prevent
their falling into Secessionist hands. The
seizure of national property in the South and
South-West had gone on. Various Federal
garrisons had been compelled to surrender.
Internal war had broken out in Missouri, in
Tennessee, from which latter State the only loyal
Southern senator, Andrew Johnson, had made
his way through difficulties and dangers of all
sorts to Washington. In Virginia the Federals
had occupied Arlington Heights, on the Virginian side of the Potomac, and various movements and skirmishes had taken place on the
border, including a somewhat disastrous one
(to the Federals) at Big Bethel (June 10). On
the other hand, the North had responded enthu-
siastically to the call for men, and forty Western
counties of Virginia had refused to follow the

remainder of the State into secession, and had organised themselves into a new loyal State, under the name of " Western Virginia."

The President in his Message, after a brief summary of the proceedings of the Secessionists to the bombardment of Fort Sumter, pointed out that this act was in no sense a matter of self-defence upon the part of the assailants :—

" They knew—they were expressly notified —that the giving of bread to the few brave and hungry men of the garrison was all which would on that occasion be attempted, unless themselves, by resisting so much, should provoke more. They knew that their Government desired to keep the garrison in the fort, not to assail them, but to maintain visible possession, and thus to preserve the Union from actual and immediate dissolution—trusting, as hereinbefore stated, to time, discussion, and the ballot-box for final adjustment ; and they assailed and reduced the fort for precisely the reverse object —to drive out the visible authority of the Federal Union, and thus force it to immediate dissolution. . . . In this act, discarding all else, they have forced upon the country the distinct issue, ' immediate dissolution or blood.' "

Rising now at once to the highest political considerations, Mr. Lincoln proceeds :—

" And this issue embraces more than the fate of these United States. It presents to the whole family of man the question, whether a constitutional republic or democracy—a government of the people by the same people—can or cannot maintain its territorial integrity against its own domestic foes. It presents the question, whether discontented individuals, too few in number to control administration, according to organic law, in any case, can always, upon the pretences made in this case, or on any other pretences, or arbitrarily, without any pretence, break up their Government. . . . It forces us to ask, ' Is there, in all republics, this inherent and fatal weakness ? Must a Government, of necessity, be too strong for the liberties of its people, or too weak to maintain its own existence ?'

So viewing the issue, no choice was left but to call out the war-power of the Government, and so to resist force employed for its destruction, by force for its preservation."

He then proceeded to review the course of events since the fall of Sumter; dwelt for a while on one of his acts which had been most sharply canvassed, the suspension of the writ of *Habeas Corpus;* and, after explaining his own views as to the right interpretation of the Constitution on the matter, deferred it entirely to the better judgment of Congress (which, it may be added at once, fully endorsed the course taken by him, and eventually passed a law authorising the President to suspend the writ "at such times and in such places, and with regard to such persons as in his judgment the public safety" might require); and closed with a somewhat lengthened discussion of the alleged " right of secession."

" It might seem, at first thought, to be of little difference whether the present movement at the South be called ' secession ' or ' rebellion.'

The movers, however, well understand the difference. At the beginning, they knew they could never raise their treason to any respectable magnitude by any name which implies violation of law. . . . They invented an ingenious sophism, which, if conceded, was followed by perfectly logical steps, through all the incidents, to the complete destruction of the Union. The sophism itself is, that any State of the Union may, consistently with the national Constitution, and therefore lawfully and peaceably, withdraw from the Union, without the consent of the Union, or of any other State. The little disguise, that the supposed right is to be exercised only for just cause, themselves to be the sole judges of its justice, is too thin to merit any notice. With rebellion thus 'sugar-coated,'* they have been drugging the public

* Mr. J. B. Carpenter, in his interesting " Anecdotes and Reminiscences of President Lincoln," appended to Mr. Raymond's work, tells us that Mr. Defrees, the Government printer, found fault with this expression, whilst the Message was passing through the press, and

E

mind of their section for more than thirty years, and until at length they have brought many good men to a willingness to take up arms against the Government, the day after some assemblage of men have enacted the farcical pretence of taking their State out of the Union, who could have been brought to no such thing the day before. . . . It is not contended that there is any express law for it; and nothing should ever be implied as law which leads to unjust or absurd consequences. · The nation purchased with money the countries out of which several of these States were formed ; is it just that they shall go off without leave and without refunding ? . . . If one State may secede, so may another ; and when all shall have seceded, none is left to pay the debts. Is this quite just to

being on intimate terms with Mr. Lincoln, remonstrated with him on the use of it as being " undignified." " Defrees," said Mr. Lincoln, " that word expresses precisely my idea, and I am not going to change it. The time will never come in this country when the people won't know exactly what *sugar-coated* means !"

creditors? Did we notify them of this sage
view of ours when we borrowed their money?
If we now recognize this doctrine by allowing
the seceders to go in peace, it is difficult to see
what we can do, if others choose to go, or to
extort terms upon which they will promise to
remain."

After asking what better Government the
country were likely to get than the present one,
and declaring that this was "essentially a
people's contest—a struggle for maintaining
in the world that form and substance of Government whose leading object is to elevate the
condition of men, to lift artificial weights from all
shoulders, to clear the paths of laudable pursuits
for all, to afford all an unfettered start and a
fair chance in the race of life," he continued :—

"Our popular Government has often been
called an experiment. Two points in it our
people have already settled—the successful establishing and the successful administering of it.
One still remains,—its successful maintenance

E 2

against a formidable internal attempt to overthrow it. It is now for them to demonstrate to
the world that those who can fairly carry an
election can also suppress a rebellion; that
ballots are the rightful and peaceful successors
of bullets; and that when ballots have fairly
and constitutionally decided, there can be no
successful appeal back to bullets. . . . Such
will be a great lesson of peace; teaching men
that what they cannot take by an election,
neither can they take by a war; teaching all
the folly of being the beginners of a war. . . .
It was with the deepest regret that the Executive
found the duty of employing the war-power in
defence of the Government forced upon him. . . .
He felt that he had no moral right to shrink, *or*
even to count the chances of his own life, in what
might follow. In full view of his great responsibility, he has so far done what he has
deemed his duty. You will now, according to
your own judgment, perform yours. . . . And
having thus chosen our course, without guile
and with pure purpose, let us renew our trust

in God, and go forward without fear and with manly hearts."

The fall of Sumter had been the answer of the South to the pleadings for concord of the President's "Inaugural." Its triumph at Bull Run (July 21) seemed to many a victorious refutation of the arguments of his first message against the right of Secession. The "Sumter" swept the West Indian seas of Federal merchant-.men. Confederate batteries at Acquia Creek almost blockaded the Potomac, and stopped communication by sea with Washington. The civil war in Missouri continued with varying success. The loyalists of East Tennessee. fled in numbers from a Confederate reign of terror, only "Parson Brownlow" in his journal, the *Knoxville Whig*, still proclaiming Unionist principles. Faithful Western Virginia, repeatedly invaded, had to be repeatedly cleared of Confederate invaders by M'Clellan, by Rosecranz. Kentucky, on the other hand, was inclining more and more to the Union. And a future series of Federal lodgments on the sea coast of the revolted States was inaugurated by the successful occupation of Hatteras Inlet in North Carolina (28th August).

The war was thus fully engaged ; by the South to destroy the Union, by the North to maintain it. But how was it to be maintained ? By respecting and protecting slavery, on which the Southern Confederacy was founded, or by striking that Confederacy through slavery itself? General Butler's ingenious application to slaves of the principle of " contraband of war," had, at an early period, (May 27), commenced an attack upon the "patriarchal institution." Absurd it certainly would have been to return fugitive slaves to disloyal owners. Accordingly, General Butler had been authorised (May 30) to retain and employ such fugitives. Subsequently (August 6), an Act was passed, forfeiting the services of all slaves " required or permitted to take up arms . . . or to work or be employed in any military or naval service whatsoever," against the United States. The right of property in slaves as against the nation was thus abolished : but not slavery itself; the master's privilege was destroyed, but no right was given to the slave. General Fremont, in command in Missouri, thought he could go further. By proclamation (August 31), he instituted martial law throughout his department, and declared that the slaves of persons taking an active part against the Government should be " free men."

Mr. Lincoln disallowed this step (Sept. 11, 1861). The motives of the act seem to have been twofold—First : an anxiety not to travel, if possible, one inch beyond the letter of the law in the matter ; Second : an equal anxiety not to outstrip public feeling generally, and especially that of the Border States. Perhaps Mr. Lincoln miscalculated the strength of the Unionist sentiment on the one side, and of the Abolitionist sentiment on the other. But even were it so, who shall dare condemn him ? To every thinking man, the mere confiscation of the slaves of rebels contained a pledge of future emancipation. Was it worth while, for the sake of hastening by a few months the fulfilment of that pledge, to peril the cause of the Union, at a time when no one signal success had given lustre to its banners? What if the allowance of General Fremont's order had thrown all the Border States at once into secession? Can we undervalue that peril, when we look back and see that the single one of those Border States which actually seceded, Virginia, has been practically the only resistent element in the Confederacy? that when, after setting the whole Federal power at defiance for four years, she was finally conquered, she carried the whole Secession with her in her fall?

A few months later (Nov. 1), the faithful old Virginian, General Scott, gave up the command-in-chief of the United States armies, and it was conferred on General M'Clellan, who seemed to be pointed out by the public voice as the fittest man for that position; partly, perhaps, through the prominence which he had acquired as United States Commissioner during the Crimean War, and partly through a late successful campaign in

Western Virginia. Another successful and momentous lodgment was effected by the Federals on the Southern coast, at Port Royal and Beaufort, South Carolina (31st Oct. to Nov. 7), and subsequently at other spots in the vicinity, and another one at Ship Island, off the Louisiana coast (3rd Dec.); and a couple of Virginian counties on a detached spit of land, (Accomac and Northampton) submitted to Federal rule. Civil war continued to rage in Missouri, Kentucky, and Tennessee,—with especial fury in the last, where the Unionist "rebels" of East Tennessee but rarely found quarter with their opponents; and a most serious complication with England arose, through the seizure (Nov. 8), by Captain Wilkes, of Messrs. Mason and Slidell, the Confederate Commissioners, from on board the English mail-steamer Trent. In spite of the popular clamour (especially of all covert friends of the South), which endorsed the act, President Lincoln took upon himself to disallow it, and the Confederate Commissioners were given up.

It was under these circumstances that Congress met for its ordinary session (Dec. 2, 1861). In his first "annual" Message, after referring, in terms of perfect moderation, to the relations of the United States with foreign nations, and to various questions of national defence and internal communication, Mr. Lincoln thus expressed himself on a matter of small practical moment, but of vast importance in principle :—

"If any good reason exists why we should persevere longer in withholding our recognition of the independence and sovereignty of Hayti and Liberia, I am unable to discern it. Unwilling, however, to inaugurate a novel policy in regard to them without the approbation of Congress, I submit for your consideration the expediency of an appropriation for maintaining a *chargé d'affaires* near each of these new States."

Let us pause for a moment to see what this means. Hayti and Liberia are two self-governed negro republics, the one of revolted, the other of enfranchised slaves. The United States had not as yet recognised either (although the latter had been founded by their own citizens), as worthy of diplomatic notice. According to the principles of the new Confederacy, they could not be so recognised. " Its foundations are laid," had said V. P. Stephens, " its corner-stone rests upon the great truth that the negro is not equal to the white man ; that slavery, subordination to the superior race, is his natural and normal condition." Mr. Lincoln, on the contrary, was "unable to discern any good reason " why negro republics should not stand on a footing of equal sovereignty with any polity founded by the white man. In the eyes of the Illinois rail-splitter, bargee, village at-torney, " slavery, subordination to the superior race," was not " the natural and normal condi-tion" of the negro. He was entitled to freedom, if he could win it—by arms if need be—and in freedom to self-government. Did not the man who had lately disallowed General Fremont's proclamation for enfranchising those slaves whom the law only declared to be confiscated, thus sufficiently vindicate his own consistency ?

Nor was this all. Referring to the Confiscation Act itself, to the numbers of confiscated
slaves, who by its operation were "already de-
pendent on the United States," and who "must
be provided for in some way," and to the possibility "that some of the States will pass
similar enactments for their own benefit re-
spectively, and by operation of which persons
of the same class will be thrown upon them for
disposal," he proceeded to indicate the first out-
lines of the policy which he afterwards earnestly,
but only in part successfully, urged upon Congress; recommending that confiscated slaves
should be deemed free, but that steps should
be taken to colonize them "in some place or
places in a climate congenial to them," the free
coloured people already in the United States
being encouraged to join in such colonization.
Hints of yet broader measures were indeed
already thrown out. "The Union must be
preserved, and hence, all indispensable means
must be employed. We should not be in haste
to determine that radical and extreme measures

which may reach the loyal as well as the disloyal, are indispensable." What was this, but
a guarded warning that universal emancipation
might become in time "indispensable?"

Next follows a vivid sketch of the progress of
the war since the assault on Fort Sumter—a
model, in my judgment, of vivid political narra-
tive :—

"The last ray of hope for preserving the
Union peaceably, expired at the assault upon
Fort Sumter, and a general review of what has
occurred since may not be unprofitable. What
was painfully uncertain then is much better
defined and more distinct now; and the progress
of events is plainly in the right direction. The
insurgents confidently claimed a strong support
from North of Mason and Dixon's line; and the
friends of the Union were not free from appre-
hension on the point. This, however, was soon
settled definitely, and on the right side. South
of the line, noble little Delaware led off right
from the first. Maryland was made to seem
against the Union. Our soldiers were assaulted,

bridges were burned, and railroads torn up within her limits; and we were many days, at one time, without the ability to bring a single regiment over her soil to the capital. Now her bridges and railroads are repaired and open to the Government; she already gives seven regiments to the cause of the Union, and none to the enemy; and her people, at a regular election, have sustained the Union by a larger majority and a larger aggregate vote than they ever before gave to any candidate or any question. Kentucky, too, for some time in doubt, is now decidedly, and I think unchangeably, ranged on the side of the Union. Missouri is comparatively quiet, and I believe cannot again be overrun by the insurrectionists. These three States of Maryland, Kentucky, and Missouri, neither of which would promise a single soldier at first, have now an aggregate of not less than 40,000 in the field for the Union; while of their citizens, certainly not more than a third of that number, and they of doubtful whereabouts and doubtful existence, are in arms against it. After a somewhat bloody struggle of months, winter closes on the Union people of Western Virginia, leaving them masters of their own country."

The President concluded by insisting, as in his former message, on the Secession being "largely, if not exclusively, a war upon the first principle of popular Government—the rights of the people." And here follows a most interesting development of his views—conceived, indeed, from the stand-point of a Western American— on the relation between capital and labour :—

"There is one point, with its connections, not so hackneyed as most others, to which I ask a brief attention. It is the effort to place capital on an equal footing with, if not above labour, in the structure of Government. It is assumed that labour is available only in connection with capital; that nobody labours unless somebody else, owning capital, somehow by the use of it induces him to labour. This assumed, it is next considered whether it is best that capital shall hire labourers, and thus induce them to work by their own consent, or buy them, and drive them to it without their consent. Having proceeded so far, it is naturally concluded that all labourers are either hired labourers, or what we call slaves. And further, it is assumed that whoever is once a hired labourer, is fixed in that condition for life. . . . Both these assumptions are false, and all inferences from them are groundless.

"Labour is prior to and independent of capital. Capital is only the fruit of labour, and could never have existed if labour had not first existed. Labour is the superior of capital, and deserves much the higher consideration. Capital has its rights, which are as worthy of protection as any other rights. Nor is it denied that there is, and probably always will be, a relation between labour and capital, producing mutual benefits. The error is in assuming that the whole labour of the community exists within that relation. A few men own capital, and those few avoid labour themselves, and, with their capital, hire or buy another few to labour for them. A large majority belong to neither class—neither work

for others, nor have others working for them.
In most of the Southern States, a majority of
the whole people, of all colours, are neither
slaves nor masters; while in the Northern a
large majority are neither hirers nor hired. . . .
Again, as has already been said, there is not of
necessity any such thing as the free hired
labourer being fixed to that condition for life.
Many independent men everywhere in those
States, a few years back in their lives, were
hired labourers.   The prudent, penniless beginner in the world labours for wages for a
while, saves a surplus with which to buy tools
or land for himself, then labours for himself
another while, and at length hires another new
beginner to help him.   This is the just, and
generous, and prosperous system, which opens
the way to all, gives hope to all, and consequent
energy, and progress, and improvement of
condition to all.   No men living are more
worthy to be trusted than those who toil up
from poverty—none less inclined to take or
touch aught which they have not honestly

F

earned. Let them beware of surrendering a political power which they already possess, and which, if surrendered, will surely be used to close the door of advancement against such as they, and to fix new disabilities and burdens upon them, till all of liberty be lost."

Mr. Lincoln does not seem to have asked himself whether the God-given thews and sinews, with which the white man labours and the black, are not in fact a "capital" which must precede all labour. But if we read his reasoning on the subject by his experience, it really means this :—'I, Abraham Lincoln, who stand here as President of these United States, began life as a hired labourer. What capital I have, I made by my labour.* If I

* One morning, in the Executive Chamber, there were present a number of gentlemen, among them Mr. Seward. A point in the conversation suggesting the thought, Mr. Lincoln said :—

"Seward, you never heard, did you, how I earned my first dollar?"

"No," said Mr. Seward.

"Well," replied he, "I was about eighteen years of

have risen, why should any be hindered from
rising? Why should even the poorest black
man remain fixed for life in the condition of a
hired labourer? still less remain a slave, unable
even to own his own body?' The Confederate
General T. R. R. Cobb, of Georgia, had written
that there was " perhaps no solution of the great

age. I belonged, you know, to what they call down
South the *Scrubs;* people who do not own slaves are
nobody there. But we had succeeded in raising, chiefly
by my labour, sufficient produce, as I thought, to justify
me in taking it down the river to sell. After much
persuasion I got the consent of mother to go, and constructed a little flat-boat, large enough to take a barrel
or two of things that we had gathered, with myself and
little bundle, down to New Orleans. A steamer was
coming down the river. We have, you know, no
wharves on the Western streams ; and the custom was,
if passengers were at any of the landings, for them to
go out in a boat, the steamer stopping and taking them
on board.

"I was contemplating my new flat-boat, and wonder-
ing whether I could make it stronger or improve it in
any particular, when two men came down to the shore
in carriages with trunks, and looking at the different
boats, singled out mine, and asked, ' Who owns this?'
I answered, somewhat modestly, ' I do.' ' Will you,' said

problem of reconciling the interests of labour
and capital . . . so simple and effective as
negro slavery. By making the labourer himself
capital, the conflict ceases, and the interests
become identical." What a gulf between the
two doctrines !

The early part of the year 1862 saw considerable progress on the part of the Federals,

one of them, 'take us and our trunks to the steamer ?'
'Certainly,' said I. I was very glad to have the chance
of earning something. I supposed that each of them
would give me two or three bits. The trunks were put
on my flat-boat, the passengers seated themselves on the
trunks, and I sculled them out to the steamboat. They
got on board, and I lifted up their heavy trunks, and
put them on deck. The steamer was about to put on
steam again, when I called out that they had forgotten
to pay me. Each of them took from his pocket a silver
half dollar, and threw it on the floor of my boat. I
could scarcely believe my eyes as I picked up the money.
Gentlemen, you may think it a very little thing, and in
these days it seems to me a trifle ; but it was a most
important incident in my life. I could scarcely credit
that I, a poor boy, had earned a dollar in less than a day,
—that by honest work I had earned a dollar. The
world seemed wider and fairer before me. I was a more
hopeful and confident being from that time."

everywhere except in Virginia, where "Stonewall" Jackson was beginning to win for himself a brilliant reputation by the rapidity and boldness of his operations, generally upon the Federal lines of communication. Kentucky was cleared from all organised military resistance, except at the South-West corner. The Federal gunboats, pushing through Kentucky up the Tennessee and Cumberland rivers, into the State of Tennessee, took Fort Henry (February 6), and with the aid of the land forces under General Grant, Fort Donelson (February 16), the latter giving no fewer than 13,300 prisoners (making, with killed and wounded, a total Confederate loss of 15,067), 3,000 horses, 48 fieldpieces, 17 heavy guns, and 20,000 stand of arms,—a check to the Confederates, in a material point of view, far worse than that of Bull Run to the Federals, whose total loss on that occasion was 2,708 (of whom some 1,200 prisoners), and 28 cannon, with some thousand muskets. Nashville, the capital of Tennessee, was occupied (February 23), never again to be lost hold of. Senator Andrew Johnson was named military governor of the State. Three Union gunboats ascended the Tennessee as far as Florence, Alabama, and were well received. A further portion of the coast of North Carolina was occupied by an expedition under General Burnside, and a lodgment effected on the coast of Georgia, at Brunswick (March 2); lastly, the Federal troops, having nearly cleared Missouri, advanced into Arkansas.

In the midst of these successes, Mr. Lincoln addressed a remarkable message to Congress (March 6, 1862), recommending "the adoption of a joint resolution, which should pledge the United States to co-operate with any State adopting gradual abolition of Slavery, by giving to it pecuniary aid." Every State initiating emancipation, he urged, would be lost for ever to the proposed Southern Confederacy. Gradual and not sudden emancipation was better for all. The current expenditure of the war would soon purchase, at a fair valuation, all the slaves in any named State. The proposal set up "no claim of a right by the Federal authority to interfere with slavery within State limits." But, as he had said in December, the Union must be preserved, and hence all indispensable means must be employed, all which may obviously promise great efficiency towards ending the struggle. The pecuniary compensation tendered would be of more value to the States and private persons concerned, than would the institution and property in it, in the present aspect of affairs. He concluded with the solemn words: " In full view of my great responsibility to my God and my country, I earnestly beg the attention of Congress and the people to the subject."

It was only on the 10th of April that a joint resolution of Congress on the subject was finally approved by the President. But the feeling of the country against slavery was now rising on all sides, and this was but one of several measures directed against it. On March 13, an additional article of war expressly prohibited, under pain of dismissal, " all officers or persons in the military or naval service of the United

States . . . from employing any of the
forces under their respective commands for the
purpose of returning fugitives from service or
labour," making thus no difference between
fugitives from loyal and from disloyal owners.
On the 16th April was passed an act for the
emancipation of all slaves within the district
of Columbia, the President accompanying his
signature with a message expressive of his satisfaction, and the act being followed by another
(May 21) "providing for the education of
coloured children in the cities of Washington
and Georgetown, district of Columbia," out of
the proceeds of the taxes received from the
coloured population of these cities, and establishing perfect equality before the civil and
criminal law within the district between the
coloured man and the white. Nor can we overlook the significant fact that, for the first time .
within forty years, a convicted slaver was hung
in New York (February 21).

Still, the President retained his old anxiety
not to travel faster than the public feeling. On

the 9th May, General Hunter, in command at
Hilton Head, South Carolina, issued a proclamation declaring all slaves free within the States
of Georgia, Florida, and South Carolina. The
President, by another proclamation (May 19),
disallowed that of General Hunter, making
known " that, whether it be competent for me,
as Commander-in-Chief of the army and navy,
to declare the slaves of any State or States free;
and whether at any time, or in any case, it shall
have become a necessity indispensable to the
maintenance of the Government to exercise such
supposed power, are questions which, under my
responsibility, I reserve to myself, and which I
cannot feel justified in leaving to the decision of
commanders in the field." Recalling, moreover,
the late resolution of Congress for aiding States
which should gradually abolish slavery, he ap-
pealed in the most touching terms to the
people of the States concerned to act on a
proposal which made " common cause for a
common object, casting no reproaches upon
any." "So much good," he declared, "has

not been done by one effort in all past time, as, in the providence of God, it is now your high privilege to do. May the vast future not have to lament that you have neglected it!"

Whether he judged rightly or wrongly in the matter, in the disavowal of General Hunter, as in that of General Fremont before, we cannot but see the truly brave man, who will shirk no responsibility by casting it on third parties, who will not be the slave of outward events, will not let any subordinate officer dictate a policy to the country. Mr. Lincoln now avowedly contemplates the possibility of emancipation as a military necessity, through an exercise of the war-power. But such a question he can leave to the decision of no mere soldier; it belongs to himself only, the chosen servant of the people, its chief military as well as civil officer. Should the act become necessary, therefore, it can never come as the stepping-stone to a military despotism, since it will be that of the only soldier who is directly responsible to the people, to the civil laws of his country. But whilst thus decisively vindicating his constitutional authority, he uses the very act which he is disallowing as a warning to the slave States of the " signs of the times." Will they neglect their opportunity for gradual, assisted emancipation ? The pleading, as we all know, was in vain. " Sinners against their own souls," the seceding Slave States, which had spurned such emancipation, had to endure it sudden, uncompensated— ay, and too often in the light of their burning stacks and homesteads, at the point of their former slaves' bayonets.

But the check to General Hunter was no check, and was meant to be no check, to the progress of public feeling against slavery. Amongst a whole group of measures in this direction which immediately followed the President's proclamation, I can but notice two or three :—

On June 18, a most important act, embodying the cardinal resolution of the Chicago platform, abolished and forbade slavery throughout all the territories of the United States, present or future. A treaty between the United States and Great Britain for the suppression of the slave-trade, conceded a mutual right of search, such as America had always withheld (July 11). An act of July 17 enacted the perpetual freedom of "all slaves of persons who shall hereafter be engaged in rebellion, or shall in any way give aid and comfort thereto, escaping and taking refuge within the lines of the army,"—"all slaves captured from such persons or deserted by them, and coming under the control of the Government of the United States,—and all slaves of such persons found in any place occupied by rebel forces, and afterwards occupied by the forces of the United States." The restoration or molestation of fugitive slaves, except upon oath of the loyalty of their owners, was expressly forbidden. "No person engaged in the military or naval service of the United States," was, "under any pretence whatever," to "assume to decide on the validity of the claim of any person to the service or labour of any other person, under pain of dismissal from

the service." Lastly, under the terms of this
act and of a somewhat more explicit one of the
same date, the President was authorised to
" receive into the service of the United States,"
for any " labour or military or naval service for
which they may be found competent," and enrol
and organise, " persons of African descent ;"
" any slave of a person in rebellion rendering
any such service " to be " for ever thereafter
free, together with his mother, wife, and
children, if they also · belong to persons in
rebellion ;" but with power also to provide for
" the transportation, colonisation, and settlement, to some tropical country beyond the
limits of the United States, of such persons of
African descent, made free by the act, as may
be willing to emigrate."

Before Congress separated, Mr. Lincoln
called the representatives of the Border States
together at the White House, and addressed
them (July 12), in an earnest speech, on the
expediency of adopting his gradual emancipation plan. On the same day he sent a Message

to Congress, transmitting the draft of a bill to compensate any State which might abolish slavery within its limits. But, on the one hand, none of the Border States responded to his invitation,—only a minority of their representatives expressing their concurrence in it; —and on the other, though the President's bill was referred to a committee, no action was taken upon it in Congress.

Meanwhile, the Federal arms had been again progressing everywhere, except in Virginia. Whilst the President's Message of March 6 was being delivered, the great Western battle of Pea Ridge, Arkansas, was beginning, which, after being renewed for two successive days, ended (March 8) with the rout of the Confederates. Successes were obtained in distant New Mexico and Arizona, till now occupied by the Confederates from Texas, both of which were recovered, the latter (June) by a volunteer force from California. The great advance down the Mississippi and its valley had been steadily carried on, the Confederates successively evacuating or surrendering their works at New Madrid, Island No. 10, Fort Wright, and the city of Memphis (June 6), and the Union forces advancing as far as Vicksburg, whilst Arkansas was crossed from its North-West corner to Helena on the Mississippi (July 11), its capital, Little Rock, being temporarily occupied. By a still more gallant exploit, the forts of the Lower Mississippi (Jackson and St. Philip), after six days' bombardment, were run past by (now) Admiral Farragut, and the surrender of New Orleans and the forts was obtained (April 28). The fleet pressing upwards received the surrender of Natchez, and a portion of it actually ran past Vicksburg, which, with some outworks at Grand Gulf and Port Hudson, lower down (the latter not yet fully fortified), was the only stronghold yet remaining to the Confederates on the great river of the West. The land operations in this quarter had been equally vigorous. The fiercely contested battle of Shiloh or Pittsburgh Landing, Tennessee (April 6-7), ended on the second day by the retreat of the Confederates, leaving 3,000 dead upon the field; but the loss of the Federals was no less than 13,298, besides many pieces of cannon. They pushed on into Mississippi, occupying Corinth (May 30), whilst a lodgment was also effected in Northern Alabama, through the capture of Huntsville (April 11). Some successes were however obtained by the Confederates in Tennessee, and their dashing general, John Morgan, invaded Kentucky. On the Southern coast the town of Pensacola was occupied from Fort Pickens, which had been retained by the Federals (May 12). The occupation of the Eastern coast was extended, the Federals taking possession—in Florida (March 7), of St. Mary's, Fernandina, St. Augustine—in Georgia, of Fort Pulaski, at the entrance of the Savannah River (April 11)—in North Carolina, of Newbern (March 14), Beaufort (March 20), &c.—in South-Eastern Virginia, of Norfolk and Suffolk (May 10, 18); but a severe repulse was suffered on James Island, South Carolina, about five miles from Charleston (June 14).

But in Virginia the resistance of the Confederates was persevering and successful. In the most important naval conflict of the war, the fight of the Confederate ram "Merrimac" with the Union fleet in Hampton Roads, Virginia, the sloop "Cumberland" was sunk, the frigate "Congress" compelled to surrender and burnt, and several other vessels disabled; and the ram was only beat off by the little steam-battery "Monitor" (March 8-9); but the "Merrimac" was afterwards destroyed by the Confederates themselves (May 11), to prevent her falling into the hands of the Federals. After four months' tenure of command on the Potomac, General M'Clellan at last moved on towards Richmond; but only to find the Confederate works round Manassas Junction evacuated (March 10), their army taking up the line of the Rappahannock. He now changed his base, and commenced what is known as the campaign of the Peninsula; the final result of which was, that after a series of most bloody battles in a most unhealthy country, the earlier ones favourable to the Union cause, the latter the reverse, during which a portion of the

Federal army was once within five miles of Richmond, and the Virginia Legislature voted 200,000 dols. for the removal of women and children, M'Clellan finally fell back to the James River (July 1), up which the Union gun-boats had vainly sought to force their way past For$_t$ Darling (May 17). During this time Jackson had forced Banks in North-Western Virginia to retreat from Winchester across the Potomac, and Fremont to fall back down the Shenandoah Valley.

The dealings between the President and General M'Clellan, during the course of the events just noticed, and up to his final supersession in the chief command, fill up the greater part of one of the most painful chapters (IX.) in Mr. Raymond's book. General M'Clellan, as events have shown, was a good second-rate general, whom injudicious friends had puffed into the belief that he was a first-rate one. In organising the Federal army after the early disasters of the war, he undoubtedly showed himself most capable, and did a work which perhaps no one else could have done in his place. But as Commander-in-Chief in the field he showed himself slow, irresolute, querulous, exacting, always apt to miss the possible whilst claiming the impossible from others. A few samples will suffice. On the 25th June, his army being then outside of the Chickahominy river, General M'Clellan had written, declaring that the Confederate force was some 200,000 strong (a gross and ridiculous exaggeration), and that if he were attacked, and the result of the action were a disaster, the "responsibility could not be thrown on his shoulders, but must rest where it belongs." The President wrote back, June 26 :—

" Your three despatches of yesterday in relation, ending with the statement that you completely succeeded in making your point, are very satisfactory. The latter one suggesting the probability of your being overwhelmed by 200,000 men, and talking of to whom the responsibility will belong, pains me very much. I give you all I can, and act on the presumption

G 2

that you will do the best you can with what you have ; while you continue, ungenerously, I think, to assume that I could give you more if I would. I have omitted,—I shall omit, no opportunity to send you reinforcements whenever I can."

On the 27th, General M'Clellan was defeated at Gaines's Mill, and began his retreat by a flank march to the James River, writing the next day to the Secretary of War that he was not responsible for the result, and concluding with the incredible words : " If I save this army, I tell you plainly, that I owe no thanks to you or to any persons in Washington ; you have done your best to sacrifice this army." The President replied (June 28) :—

" Save your army at all events. Will send reinforcements as fast as we can. Of course they cannot reach you to-day, to-morrow, or next day. I have not said that you were ungenerous for saying you needed reinforcements ; I thought you were ungenerous in assuming that I did not send them as fast as I could. I feel any misfortune to you and your army quite as keenly as you feel it yourself. If you have had a drawn battle or a repulse, it is the price we pay for the enemy not being in Washington. . . . It is the nature of the case, and neither you nor the Government is to blame."

The retreat continued amid fierce fighting, not personally shared in by the general, who headed his retreating forces, telegraphing meanwhile for reinforcements. Mr. Lincoln wrote (July 1) :—

"It is impossible to reinforce you for your present emergency. If we had half-a-million of men we could not get them to you in time. We have not the men to send. If you are not strong enough to face the enemy, you must find a place of security, and wait, rest and repair. Maintain your ground if you can ; but save your army at all events, even if you fall back to Fort Monroe. We still have strength enough in the country, and will bring it out."

The General's reply was to ask for 50,000 more troops ! Nothing can exceed the patient

gentleness of the sore-tried President's answer
(July 2):—

" Your despatch of yesterday induces me to
hope that your army is having some rest. In
this hope, allow me to reason with you for a
moment. When you ask for 50,000 men to be
promptly sent you, you surely labour under
some gross mistake of fact. Recently you sent
papers showing your disposal of forces made last
spring for the defence of Washington, and ad-
vising a return to that plan. I find it included
in and about Washington 75,000 men. Now,
please be assured that I have not men enough
to fill that very plan by 50,000. . . . Thus,
the idea of sending you 50,000, or any other
considerable force promptly, is simply absurd.
If, in your frequent mention of responsibility,
you have the impression that I blame you for
not doing more than you can, please be relieved of such impression. I only beg that, in
like manner, you will not ask impossibilities
of me. If you think you are not strong enough

to take Richmond just now, I do not ask you to try just now. Save the army, material and *personnel*, and I will strengthen it for the offensive again as fast as I can. The governors of eighteen States offer me a new levy of 300,000, which I accept."

It is characteristic of Mr. Lincoln, that at a meeting on the 6th August, when M'Clellan's admirers were seeking to uphold the military reputation of their hero by throwing the whole responsibility of his failures on the Government, Mr. Lincoln simply tried to clear at once both the General and the War-Minister :—

" General M'Clellan has sometimes asked for things that the Secretary of War did not give him. General M'Clellan is not to blame for asking what he wanted and needed, and the Secretary of War is not to blame for not giving when he had none to give."

The failure of M'Clellan's attempt to take Richmond from the York River was followed by a course of events, except in the West, almost uniformly adverse to the Federals. By command of General Halleck, then General-in-Chief (August 3), General M'Clellan, though under protest, had to withdraw his army from the banks of the James, the Federals retaining only Yorktown, Williamsburg, and a strip of coast, as the results of their Peninsular campaign. General Pope, placed in command of the army, was outmanœuvred and finally defeated in a second battle of Bull Run by General Lee (Augnst 31), and threw up his command. Pushing on beyond the Potomac into Maryland and Pennsylvania, whilst Harper's Ferry, with 11,000 men, 73 guns, and a large quantity of ammunition, was surrendered to one of Jackson's subordinates, the Confederates were only checked by M'Clellan (who had been replaced in command on Pope's resignation), at South Mountain (September 14), and at Antietam (September 17), losing at the latter about 14,000 killed and wounded, and 13 guns (the Federal loss being 12,469) ; but they were allowed to retreat unmolested into Virginia. Eventually (November 5), General M'Clellan, having since October 6 delayed to comply with an express order to cross the Potomac, was superseded in favour of his friend, General Burnside. Various reverses were suffered in Tennessee and Kentucky; Cincinnati, the great business city of Ohio, was threatened; and the important position of Cumberland Gap was evacuated (September 17). Still, the successive advances into Kentucky of Morgan and Bragg were checked; and each invasion of Kentucky, as of Maryland, only proved that the majority of the population in the Border slave States, Virginia excepted, were by this time staunch to the Union. In Arkansas much fighting took place, almost invariably favourable to the Federals, as also some in South-Western Missouri and Kansas; whilst General Rosecranz won the battle of Iuka (September 19-20) and Corinth (October 1-3), in the latter of which, after a first day's success, the Confederates were defeated, with a loss of nearly 10,000 men out of 38,000. On the coast, Galveston, Texas, was occupied (October 4), though, as it turned out, only for a time; and an unsuccessful attempt was made in South Carolina to occupy the Charleston and Savannah Railroad at Pocotaligo (October 22).

But, meanwhile, the great principles on which the war turned were coming out more and more. For some time the President adhered to his scheme, towards which Congress had placed 600,000 dols. at his disposal, for colonising the coloured people abroad. Some of them entered into the scheme, and formed a committee, which was received by the President at the White House, and addressed by him (August 14) in a speech, of which notes were taken by one of those present, and which has been much canvassed. "You and we," he said, "are different races. We have between us a broader difference than exists between almost any other two races. · · · · This physical difference is a great disadvantage to us both, as I think. . . . If this is admitted, it affords a reason, at least, why we should be separated. . . . Your race are suffering, in my judgment, the greatest wrong inflicted on any people. But even when you

cease to be slaves, you are cut off from many of
the advantages which the other race enjoys.
The aspiration of man is to enjoy equality with
the best when free ; but on this broad continent
not a single man of your race is made the equal
of a single man of ours. Go where you are
treated the best, and the ban is still upon you.
. . . . I need not recount to you the effects
upon white men, growing out of the institution
of slavery. I believe in its general evil effects
on the white race. See our present condition—
the country engaged in war; our white men
cutting one another's throats, none knowing
how far it will extend. . . . But for your race
among us there could not be war, although
many men engaged on either side do not care
for you one way or the other. . . . It is better
for us both, therefore, to be separated. . . . .
There is an unwillingness on the part of our
people, harsh as it may be, for you free coloured
people to remain with us. . . . If intelligent
coloured men, such as are before me, would move
in this matter, much might be accomplished. . .
For the sake of your race you should sacrifice

something of your present comfort. . . . It is a cheering thought throughout life, that something can be done to ameliorate the condition of those who have been subject to the hard usages of the world. It is difficult to make a man miserable while he feels he is worthy of himself, and claims kindred to the great God who made him."

He then pointed out Liberia, as one field for colonisation. But "some of you would rather remain within reach of the country of your nativity. *I do not know how much attachment you may have toward our race. It does not strike me that you have the greatest reason to love them.* But still you are attached to them, at all events." So he was thinking for them of Central America. There, "all the factions are agreed alike on the subject of colonisation, and want it, and are more generous than we are here. To your coloured race they have no objection. Besides, I would endeavour to have you made equals, and have the best assurance that you should be the equals of the best." So he asked them to consider the thing seriously, "for the good of mankind."

I have never been able to find the fault with
this speech that many have,—absolutely mistaken
as I believe it to have been, in point of opinion.
The President's first duty was to the Union,
which he had to preserve so far as it existed, to
restore so far as it was broken up. The effort
to restore it, he clearly felt, led him day by day
towards the destruction of slavery. That, he
thought, could be more easily effected by the
simultaneous removal of the coloured race. Yet
he was determined,—this is implied, throughout
not only his speech to the coloured committee,
but throughout his whole conduct from first to
last,—to impose no coercion upon them for the
purpose. So he urges them to remove themselves. He addresses them with perfect candour,
not as inferiors, but as equals,—not extenuating
in anywise the wrongs which have been and are
inflicted on them,—claiming from them no
gratitude, no deference, no submission,—appealing only to their self-respect, to their wish to
benefit their fellows. They are not the equals
of the white men here; why not go where they
" should be the equals of the best ?" Evidently,

he is doing by these coloured men precisely as he would be done by. There is, in fact, the broadest assertion of human equality beneath this effort to dissociate two races, of which the one will not treat the other as its equal.

But the President's leading point of view, that of saving the Union, must never be overlooked. He set it forth himself with unmistakeable clearness in a letter of nearly the same date (August 22) to Mr. Horace Greeley, who had somewhat bitterly attacked him in the *New York Tribune:*—

"Dear Sir,—I have just read yours of the 19th instant, addressed to myself through the *New York Tribune.* If there be in it any statements or assumptions of fact which I may know to be erroneous, I do not now and here controvert them. If there be any inferences which I may believe to be falsely drawn, I do not now and here argue against them. If there be perceptible in it an impatient and dictatorial tone, I waive it in deference to an old friend, whose heart I have always supposed to be right. As to the policy I 'seem to be pursuing,' as you say, I have not meant to leave any one in doubt. I would save the Union. I would save it in the shortest way under the constitution. The sooner the national authority can be restored, the nearer the Union will be—the Union as it was.

"If there be those who would not save the Union unless they could at the same time save slavery, I do not agree with them. If there be those who would not save the Union unless they could at the same time destroy slavery, I do not agree with them. My paramount object is to save the Union, and not either to save or destroy slavery. If I could save the Union without freeing any slave, I would do it;*—if I could save it by freeing all the slaves, I would do it; —and if I could do it by freeing some and leaving others alone, I would also do that.

* A *Times'* correspondent, referring obviously to this passage, recently spoke of Mr. Lincoln as having "boasted" that if he could save the Union without freeing any slave, he would do it. Can there be a grosser perversion of the truth, as the whole context shows? Will calumny not spare this man even in his grave?

What I do about slavery, and the coloured race, I do because I believe it helps to save this Union; and what I forbear, I forbear because I do not believe it would help to save the Union. I shall do less whenever I shall believe what I am doing hurts the cause, and I shall do more whenever I believe doing more will help the cause. I shall try to correct errors when shown to be errors, and I shall adopt new views so fast as they shall appear to be true views. I have here stated my purpose according to my views of official duty, and I intend no modification of my oft expressed personal wish that all men everywhere could be free."

It is written :—" He that doeth truth cometh to the light, that his deeds may be made manifest, that they are wrought in God." Did ever man more resolutely than this man "come to the light, that his deeds might be made manifest?" Did ever man,—instead of, like so many other rulers, darkening counsel by words without understanding,—seek and find words which should so clearly, simply set forth the purpose of a strong, pure will, scorning all dis-

guise? Not to dwell on the sinewy, manly
English of the ex-rail-splitter, ex-bargee, beside
which the most admired samples of contemporary
"style" might well act almost as an emetic on
the reader, observe again the truly Baconian
philosophy which pervades the President's policy:
"I shall try to correct errors when shown to be
errors, and I shall adopt new views as fast as
they appear to be true views. In other words:
'I am no *doctrinaire*. I have no system to
which God's world is to be compelled to con-
form. I study the facts of that world, and shall
study them—from them to form, from them to
correct, my judgment as to means. But I have
an end, and to this end I mean to use these facts
as best I may. They are given me to govern
by studying them, not idly and blindly to follow
and obey. My end is the fulfilment of the duty
which I have accepted,—to save this Union, this
people, this commonwealth of which I am the
ruler. With the fulfilment of that duty I
will allow no wishes of mine, even the dearest
and the most righteous, to interfere,—not even

H

the wish that all men everywhere could be free.'

Did the President really believe that his duty could extend so far as to rivet the shackles of the slave? He knew that it could not, and did not. He knew that wherever the Union arms extended, slaves were being received as fugitives, confiscated, freed. He, and his Secretary of War had been issuing orders and proclamations to this effect, in accordance with recent legislation. Negro troops were being embodied on various points, from South Carolina to Kansas and New Orleans. The black men whom he had been urging to emigrate, were learning to stand shoulder to shoulder with the white man in defence of a common country. In the free North, Governor Sprague, of Rhode Island (Aug. 4), was raising and promising to head a negro regiment. The cry for immediate emancipation was rising higher and higher. On the 13th of September—Maryland being already invaded— the President received a deputation from all the religious denominations in Chicago upon the subject. As a study in mental philosophy, no speech of Mr. Lincoln's is more interesting to me than his reply to this deputation—which, nevertheless, has been singularly misunderstood. You see in it that rare type of excellence, a thoroughly judicial mind. The speech is really that of a man who, to make sure of the correctness of his own conclusions, wishes to argue out every possible objection to them. He says he has thought much on the subject for weeks, for months. Good men, religious men, men " equally certain that they represent the divine will," beset him with the most opposite opinions and advice. The one class or the other must be mistaken, "perhaps in some respect both."

" I hope it will not be irreverent for me to say, that if it is probable that God would reveal His will to others, on a point so connected with my duty, it might be supposed He would reveal it directly to me ; for, unless I am more deceived in myself than I often am, it is my earnest desire to know the will of Providence in this matter; and if I can learn what it is, I will do it. I

suppose it will be granted that I am not to
expect a direct revelation. I must study the
plain physical facts of the case, ascertain what is
possible, and learn what appears to be wise and
right. . . . Why, the rebel soldiers are pray-
ing with a great deal more earnestness, I fear,
than our own troops, and expecting God to
favour their side."

What good would a proclamation of emancipation from him do? He does "not want to
issue a document, that the whole world will see
necessarily must be inoperative, like the Pope's
bull against the comet." But after enumerating
all the arguments on this head, he interposes the
caution :— "Understand, I raise no objections
against it on legal or constitutional grounds ; for,
as Commander-in-Chief of the army and navy in
time of war, I suppose I have a right to take any
measure which may best subdue the enemy."
And after urging various other objections, he
concludes by a second caution, which reveals the
whole man :—

"Do not misunderstand me because I have
mentioned these objections. They indicate the

difficulties that have thus far prevented my action in some such way as you desire. I have not decided against a proclamation of liberty to the slaves, but hold the matter under advisement; and I can assure you that the subject is on my mind by day and night, more than any other. Whatever shall appear to be God's will, I will do."

Nine days more elapsed; South Mountain was fought, then Antietam (Sept. 17), and on the 22nd, the President issued his first Emancipation Proclamation, announcing that, "On the 1st day of January, 1863, all persons held as slaves within any State, or designated part of a State, the people whereof shall then be in rebellian against the United States, shall be then, thenceforward, and for ever, free."

Mr. F. B. Carpenter has given to the world the history of the Emancipation Proclamation, as related by Mr. Lincoln himself, in familiar conversation, to the writer:—

"It had got to be Midsummer, 1862. Things had gone on from bad to worse, until I felt that

we had reached the end of our rope on the plan
of operations we had been pursuing; that we
had about played our last card, and must change
our tactics or lose the game.   I now determined
upon the adoption of the Emancipation policy;
and without consultation with, or the knowledge
of, the Cabinet, I prepared the original draft
of the proclamation, and, after much anxious
thought, called a Cabinet meeting upon the
subject.   This was the last of July, or the first
part of the month of August, 1862 (the exact
date he did not remember).   This Cabinet
meeting took place, I think, upon a Saturday.
All were present, excepting Mr. Blair, the
Postmaster-General, who was absent at the
opening of the discussion, but came in subsequently.   I said to the Cabinet that I had resolved upon this step, and had not called them
together to ask their advice, but to lay the
subject-matter of a proclamation before them;
suggestions as to which would be in order, after
they had heard it read. . . . Various suggestions were offered.   Secretary Chase wished the

language stronger in reference to the arming of
the blacks. Mr. Blair, after he came in, deprecated the policy, on the ground that it would
cost the Administration the fall [*i.e.*, autumn]
elections. Nothing, however, was offered that
I had not already fully anticipated in my own
mind, until Secretary Seward spoke. Said he,
' Mr. President, I approve of the proclamation,
but I question the expediency of its issue at this
juncture. The depression of the public mind,
consequent upon our repeated reverses, is so
great, that I fear the effect of so important a
step. It may be viewed as the last measure of
an exhausted Government,—a cry for help ;
the Government stretching forth its hands to
Ethiopia, instead of Ethiopia stretching forth
her hands to the Government. His idea was,
that it would be considered our last *shriek* on
the retreat. Now,' continued Mr. Seward,
' while I approve the measure, I suggest, sir,
that you postpone its issue until you can give it
to the country supported by military success,
instead of issuing it, as would be the case now,

upon the greatest disasters of the war.' The
wisdom of the view of the Secretary of State
struck me with very great force. It was an
aspect of the case that, in all my thought upon
the subject, I had entirely overlooked. The
result was, that I put the draft of the proclamation aside, as you do your sketch for a picture,
waiting for a victory. From time to time I
added or enlarged a line, touching it up here
and there, waiting the progress of events. Well,
the next news we had was of Pope's disaster at
Bull Run. Things looked darker than ever.
Finally came the week of the battle of Antietam,
and I determined to wait no longer. The news
came, I think, on Wednesday, that the advantage was on our side. I was then staying at the
Soldiers' Home (three miles out of Washington). Here I finished writing the second draft
of the preliminary proclamation ; came up on
Saturday, called the Cabinet together to hear it,
and it was published the following Monday."

But Mr. Lincoln, always reticent as to his
deepest sources of feeling, did not tell the

young artist that which he learnt from a member of the Cabinet :—

"Mr. Chase told me, that at the Cabinet meeting immediately after the battle of Antietam, and just prior to the issue of the September Proclamation, the President entered upon the business before them, by saying that the time for the annunciation of the Emancipation policy could no longer be delayed. Public sentiment, he thought, would sustain it, many of his warmest friends and supporters demanded it, *and he had promised his God that he would do it.* The last part of this was uttered in a low tone, and appeared to be heard by no one but Secretary Chase, who was sitting near him. He asked the President if he correctly understood him? Mr. Lincoln replied, 'I made a solemn vow before God, that if General Lee were driven back from Pennsylvania, I would crown the result by the declaration of freedom to the slaves.'"

The governors of fourteen loyal States, and the proxies from three others, in a meeting at

Altoona, expressed their hearty assent to the proclamation (Sept. 24). The President was on the same day serenaded at Washington, and acknowledged the compliment in a short speech, stating that what he had done he had done "after a very full deliberation, and under a heavy and solemn sense of responsibility," trusting in God he had "made no mistake," declining "to sustain" what he had "done or said by any comment," but, according to his wont, turning away all praise from himself to "all good and brave officers and men" who had fought the late successful battles.

A proclamation for the orderly observance of the Sabbath deserves much to be noticed (Nov. 16). "The President, Commander-in-Chief of the army and navy, desires and enjoins the orderly observance of the Sabbath by the officers and men in the military and naval service. The importance for man and beast of the prescribed weekly rest, the sacred rights of Christian soldiers and sailors, a becoming deference to the best sentiment of a Christian people, and a due regard for the divine will, demand that Sunday labour in the army and navy be reduced to the measure of strict necessity. The discipline and character of the national forces should not suffer, nor the cause they defend be imperilled, by the profanation of the day or name of the Most High. . . . The first general order issued by the Father of his country [Washington], after the Declaration of Independence, indicates the spirit in which our institutions were founded, and should ever be defended : ' The General hopes and trusts that every officer and man will endeavour to live and act as becomes a Christian soldier defending the dearest rights and liberties of his country.' "

I pass to Mr. Lincoln's second annual Message (Dec. 1), far too long indeed. to be analyzed, still less commented on at length. In proceeding to the subject of " compensated emancipation," the President said :—

" A nation may be said to consist of its territory, its people, and its laws. The territory is the only part which is of certain durability.

' One generation passeth away, and another generation cometh, but the earth abideth for ever.' . . . That portion of the earth's surface which is owned and inhabited by the people of the United States, is well adapted for the home of one national family; and it is not well adapted for two or more. Its vast extent, and its variety of climate and productions, are of advantage in this age for one people, whatever they might have been in former ages. Steam, telegraphs, and intelligence have brought these to be an advantageous combination for one united people. . . . There is no line, straight or crooked, suitable for a national boundary upon which to divide. Trace through, from East to West, upon the line between the free and slave country, and we shall find a little more than one-third of its length are rivers, easy to be crossed, and populated, or soon to be populated, thickly on both sides; while nearly all its remaining length are merely surveyors' lines, over which people may walk back and forth without any consciousness of their presence. . . . But

there is another difficulty. The great interior
region, bounded East by the Alleghanies, North
by the British dominions, West by the Rocky
Mountains, and South by the line along which
the culture of corn and cotton meets, and which
includes part of Virginia, part of Tennessee, all
of Kentucky, Ohio, Indiana, Michigan, Wisconsin, Illinois, Missouri, Kansas, Iowa, Minnesota,
and the territories of Dakota, Nebraska, and
part of Colorado, already have above ten
millions of people, and will have fifty millions
within fifty years, if not prevented by any
political folly or mistake. It contains more than
one-third of the country owned by the United
States,—certainly more than a million of square
miles. . . . A glance at the map shows that,
territorially speaking, it is the great body of the
Republic. The other parts are but marginal
borders to it. . . . In the production of provisions, grains, grasses, and all which proceed
from them, this great interior region is naturally
one of the most important of the world. . . .
And yet this region has no sea-coast, touches

no ocean anywhere. As part of one nation, its people now find, and may for ever find, their way to Europe by New York, to South America and Africa by New Orleans, and to Asia by San Francisco. But separate our common country into two nations, as designed by the present rebellion, and every man of this great interior region is thereby cut off from some one or more of these outlets, not perhaps by a physical barrier, but by embarrassing and onerous trade regulations. . . . These outlets, East, West, and South, are indispensable to the well-being of the people inhabiting and to inhabit this vast interior region. . . . They will not ask where a line of separation shall be, but will vow rather that there shall be no such line. Nor are the marginal regions less interested in these communications to and through them to the great outside world. They too, and each of them, must have access to this Egypt of the West, without paying toll at the crossing of any national boundary. Our national strife springs not from our permanent part, not from the land

we inhabit; not from our national homestead.
. . . In all its adaptations and aptitudes it
demands union, and abhors separation. In fact
it would ere long force re-union, however much
of blood and treasure the separation might have
cost. Our strife pertains to ourselves,—to the
passing generations of men,—and it can, without convulsion, be hushed for ever with the
passing of one generation."*

I must say it seems to me that it would be
difficult to find more thoughtful and broader
statesmanship than is shown by this portion of
the message, which the *Times*, followed by well-
nigh the whole of the penny-a-lining crew,
chose to make game of. I see before me a man
who not only looks straight at things,—a very

---

* Surely Dr. Storrs, in his noble " Oration commemorative of Abraham Lincoln," (Brooklyn, 1865), must
have forgotten this message, when he said that Mr. Lincoln
seems hardly to have thought of the vast expanse of the
country, "with its prodigal progress in wealth, population,
and all resources . . . and was scarcely sustained or moved
in his work by any condition derived from them." (See
pp. 27-8.)

rare gift already,—but tries to look them through and through, and to form his own conclusions upon them. He is not in this respect unlike our own Prince Albert, only with rougher powers, which have to be exerted, under terrible emergencies, upon mightier subjects.

Mr. Lincoln then proceeded to develope his plan for compensated emancipation, by payments from the Federal Government to every State which should abolish slavery before the 1st January, 1900,—"all slaves who should have enjoyed actual freedom by the chances of the war, at any time before the end of the rebellion," to be nevertheless ",for ever free," but with compensation to their (loyal) owners. On this plan I need not dwell. None, perhaps, but Mr. Lincoln believed in the possibility of its being adopted. Nay, from what he says on the subject of the colonization of the coloured race, it is evident that he was himself beginning to lose faith in his pet notion of their voluntary expatriation,—facing resolutely the possibility of their remaining:—

" There is an objection urged against free
coloured persons remaining in the country,
which is largely imaginary, if not sometimes
malicious. It is insisted that their presence
would injure and displace white labour and
white labourers. If there ever could be a proper
time for mere catch arguments, that time surely
is not now. *In times like the present men should
utter nothing for which they would not willingly be
responsible through time and in eternity.* Is it true,
then, that coloured people can displace any more
white labour by being free than by remaining
slaves? If they stay in their old places they
jostle no white labourers ; if they leave their old
places they leave them open to white labourers.
. . . Emancipation, even without deportation,
would probably enhance the wages of white
labour, and very surely would not reduce them.
. . . But it is dreaded that the freed people
will swarm forth and cover the whole land. Are
they not already in the land ? Will liberation
make them any more numerous ? Equally distributed among the whites of the whole country

I

there would be but one coloured to seven whites.
. . . There are many communities now having
more than one free coloured person to seven
whites ; and this without any apparent consciousness of evil from it. The district of Columbia
and the States of Maryland and Delaware are all
in this condition. . . . But why should emancipation south send the freed people north?
People of any colour seldom run unless there be
something to run from."

After carefully pointing out that neither " the
war nor proceedings under the emancipation
proclamation" would be stayed because of the
recommendation of his plan, and after apologiz-
ing for his own insistence, Mr. Lincoln concluded with the following weighty words :—

' " Fellow-citizens, we cannot escape history.
We of this congress and this administration will
be remembered in spite of ourselves. . . . The
fiery trial through which we pass will light us
down, in honour or dishonour, to the latest
generation. We say that we are for the Union.
The world will not forget that we say this. We

know how to save the Union. The world
knows we do know how to save it. We—even
we here—hold the power and bear the responsibility. In giving freedom to the slave we
assure freedom to the free—honourable alike in
what we give and what we preserve. We shall
nobly save or meanly lose the last best hope of
earth. Other means may succeed; this could
not, cannot fail. The way is plain, peaceful,
generous, just,—a way which, if followed, the
world will for ever applaud, and God must for
ever bless."

" Plain " and " peaceful " the plan might be
called ; " generous " to the slaveholders, it
certainly was. Was it altogether "just " to the
slave ? Was it right that the loyalty of certain
slave States should be paid for, in the first
instance, at their slaves' expense ? compensated
by the bondage of a whole generation of the
coloured race in those States ? I am persuaded
that such an extension of the duration of slavery
in the loyal States formed part neither of Mr.
Lincoln's purpose nor of his expectations. With

slavery abolished under the proclamation in any
States remaining in revolt—with the strength
given to the abolitionist feeling in the North
by the war,—with the raising of the status of
the coloured man by various measures of recent
legislation, but above all, through his enrolment
in the ranks of the army,—it was utterly impossible that slavery should long hold its ground
in any State remaining loyal, or returning to its
allegiance. Yet, in proposing such a plan, I
believe Mr. Lincoln did to some extent sacrifice
principle to expediency. His old reverence for
Henry Clay perhaps betrayed him into urging
compromise, when the times called for high
assertion of the right. At any rate the attempt
failed. The Border States still would not eman-
cipate. The Free States would not bribe them
to do so. And so the war rolled on towards
the fated 1st January, 1863.

Not by any means with credit to the Federal
arms. Few single months of the struggle saw
more disasters than December, 1862. The
terrible failure of Burnside before the Confederate
works of Fredericksburg, (December 13) with a

Unionist loss of 1,512 killed and 6,000 wounded,* followed by a fresh withdrawal of the Federal army beyond the Rappahannock, and a new dash of Confederate cavalry into Maryland (which however proved a mere raid);—the scarcely less terrible repulse of Sherman before Vicksburg (26-29) followed by the temporary withdrawal of the army from its neighbourhood, and Sherman's own supersession by M'Clernand, —a few days previously (December 19) the surrender of Holly Springs, Mississippi, to the Confederates, with 2,000,000 dollars' worth of stores (an event which compelled General Grant to fall back, and thereby prevented him from co-operating with Sherman, whilst enabling the Confederates to throw reinforcements into Vicksburg)—the capture of three whole regiments and a party of cavalry, by Morgan's guerrillas at Hartsville, Tennessee (December 7), —and other smaller mishaps,. were not suffi-

* The President is reported to have said on this occasion : " If there is a man out of perdition that suffers more than I do, I pity him."

ciently set off by successes in Arkansas, an advance of General Foster in North Carolina, which led to nothing, and the hardly contested battle of Murfreesborough in Tennessee, which began on the 31st by the defeat of General M'Cook, and only terminated on January 4 by the retreat of the Confederates. At sea, while the Alabama was continuing her depredations on the coast of Cuba, the Monitor, the single Federal vessel which had won a distinct name hitherto, foundered a little before the last midnight of the year.

It was under these circumstances that the President had to fulfil his pledge given in September, 1862, and to issue, on the 1st of January, 1863, his famous proclamation, whereby, in virtue of the power vested in him as " Commander-in-Chief of the army and navy of the United States in time of actual armed rebellion against the authority and Government of the United States, and as a fit and necessary war measure for suppressing the said rebellion," he designates as being in rebellion the States of

Arkansas, Texas, Louisiana (thirteen counties excepted), Mississippi, Alabama, Florida, Georgia, South Carolina, North Carolina, and Virginia (the forty-eight counties of Western Virginia, and seven others, excepted), and ordered and declared :—

" That all persons held as slaves within said designated States, and parts of States, are and henceforward shall be free ; and that the Executive Government of the United States, including the military and naval authorities thereof, will recognize and maintain* the freedom of said persons. And I hereby enjoin upon the people so declared to be free, to abstain from all violence, unless in necessary self-defence ; and I recommend to them that, in all cases where allowed, they labour faithfully for reasonable wages. And I further declare and make known that such persons, of suitable condition, will be received into the armed service of the United States to garrison forts, positions, stations, and

---

* The words " and maintain," are due to Mr. Seward.

other places, and to man vessels of all sorts in said service. And upon this act, sincerely believed to be an act of justice, warranted by the Constitution upon military necessity, I invoke the considerate judgment of mankind, and the gracious favour of Almighty God."*

The exact bearing of this step should not be exaggerated. Mr. Lincoln proclaimed the slaves within the rebellious States free: he did not abolish slavery therein. To do this would have altogether transcended even his war powers as Commander-in-Chief, which might, however, authorise the enfranchisement of all slaves existing at a given period within certain limits, such enfranchisement being practically only a peculiar form of confiscation of a peculiar kind of property. Yet this would no more hinder the inhabitants of the States in question from purchasing other slaves, and exercising over them, the war once ended, all powers given by the local

* This last sentence is due to Mr. Chase, with the exception of the words " upon military necessity," inserted by Mr. Lincoln.

or general law over slaves generally, than a confiscation of all horses and mules within the same limits would have hindered them from buying other animals of the same description, and saddling or harnessing them at pleasure. The proclamation could thus be no more than a beginning of the good work, to be completed in every case by State action. Nor indeed did it or could it apply to the loyal Slave States— Delaware, Maryland, Kentucky, Missouri, with the excepted portions of Virginia and Louisiana, besides Tennessee. Slavery was thus left subsisting over an area which, at the Census of .1860, had contained between seven and eight hundred thousand human chattels; although that figure had been enormously reduced by the various events of the war—emigration South of planters with their slaves, escapes, confiscations.

Still, the great word had been spoken. Upwards of 3,000,000 of slaves were declared entitled to immediate freedom. The chief magistrate of the United States proclaimed to his countrymen, to the world, that the freedom of these 3,000,000 was not merely involved in the maintenance of the American Union, but was essential to it. Henceforth, none but the helplessly or wilfully blind could fail to see that the cause of freedom, in the great conflict which was raging on the American Continent, was the cause of the North.

CHAPTER III.

THE Emancipation Proclamation was warmly
received by all in Europe whose sympathy with
human freedom was genuine, and who had not
suffered themselves to be misled by sophisms
and mis-statements. The working men of Manchester, amongst others,—in the very midst of
the cotton famine,—had met on the 31st December, and forwarded to the President a congratulatory address. His reply (January 19th,
1863), might well deserve to be quoted at full
length. He indicated, as "the key" to all the
past and future measures of his administration,
the duty "to maintain and preserve at once the
constitution and the integrity of the Federal
republic." He had well understood, "that the

duty of self-preservation rests solely with the American people." But he knew that "favour or disfavour of foreign nations might have a material influence in enlarging or prolonging the struggle." He had especially expected that "if justice and good faith should be practised by the United States, they would encounter no hostile influence on the part of Great Britain.

"It is now a pleasant duty to acknowledge the demonstration you have given of your desire that a spirit of amity and peace toward this country may prevail in the councils of your Queen, *who is respected and esteemed in your own country only more than she is by the kindred nation which has its home on this side of the Atlantic.* I know, and deeply deplore, the sufferings which the working men at Manchester, and in all Europe, are called to endure in this crisis. It has been often and studiously represented that the attempt to overthrow this Government, which was built upon the foundation of human rights, and to substitute for it one which should rest exclusively on the basis of human slavery,

was likely to obtain the favour of Europe. . . .
Under the circumstances, I cannot but regard
your decisive utterances upon the question as
*an instance of sublime Christian heroism, which
has not been surpassed in any age or in any
country.* It is indeed an energetic and rein-
spiring assurance of the inherent power of truth,
and of the ultimate and universal triumph of
justice, humanity, and freedom. I do not doubt
that the sentiments you have expressed will be
sustained by your great nation ; and on the
other hand, I have no hesitation in assuring you
that they will excite admiration, esteem, and
the most reciprocal feelings of friendship, among
the American people. I hail this interchange
of sentiment, therefore, as an augury that whatever else may happen, whatever misfortune may
befall your country or my own, the peace and
friendship which now exist between the two
nations will be, as it shall be my desire to make
them, perpetual."

Does the above need any comment?*

* To this period also belongs a letter to a member of

The session of Congress closed on the 4th of
March, after having passed various measures for
strengthening the hands of the President, and
for the vigorous prosecution of the war, including
a bill authorising a draft of the militia of the
whole country.   It was well for Mr. Lincoln
that he possessed this support in Congress; for,
with the exception of Grant's movements in the
valley of the Mississippi, the first six months
of 1863 were among the gloomiest of the war.
Burnside having been relieved (24th of January)
in the command of the army of the Potomac by
Hooker,—" Fighting Joe Hooker,"—a dashing
general of division, who had been among the

the " United States Christian Commission," over a meeting of which Mr. Lincoln had been invited to preside (Feb.
22), of which the following is an extract :—" Whatever
shall tend to turn our thoughts from the unreasoning
and, uncharitable passions, prejudices, and jealousies
incident to a great national trouble such as ours, and to
fix them on the vast and long-enduring consequences,
for weal or for woe, which are to result from the struggle,
and especially to strengthen our reliance on the Supreme
Being for the final triumph of the right, cannot but be
well for us all."

sharpest critics of M'Clellan's caution and inde-
cision, on the 27th of April he too began his
advance to Richmond, but only to meet with
new disasters, and to fall back again to the North
of the Rappahannock after the bloody battles of
Chancellorsville (2-5 May), with a loss of not
far from 18,000 men. In the West, Vicksburg
for several months bade defiance to the Federals.
They took various forts on neighbouring rivers;
they tried to divert the course of the Mississippi
from under its walls; but all efforts failed, until,
on the 30th of April, Grant commenced a new
movement, by landing his forces sixty-five miles
lower down the river, and then marching up,
which compelled the evacuation by the Confederates of some strong fortifications at Grand
Gulf, dispersed the forces which, under General
Joseph Johnstone, were advancing to relieve
the place, threw the city of Jackson, capital of
the State of Mississippi, with large stores of
supplies, into the temporary occupation of the
Federals, deprived the garrison, which had
advanced out to meet the Federals, of a large

portion of its artillery, and ended by the close
investment of Vicksburg itself, 18th of May;
but an attempt to carry the place by storm
failed again, and a regular siege had to be
opened.

Internal dissensions in the North added to
the gloom of ill-success. To say nothing of a
struggle of factions in Missouri, tormenting the
President, as he wrote himself, " beyond endur-
ance," the Democratic party throughout the
country was seriously thwarting the action of
the Government. Its most prominent spokes-
man at this time was Mr. Vallandigham, of
Ohio, an old pro-slavery man, who had rejoiced
over John Brown's execution. He declared the
war to be waged for the freedom of the blacks
and the enslaving of the whites, accused the
Government of having deliberately rejected pro-
positions which would have brought the South
back into the Union, proclaimed his intention to
disobey a certain order of General Burnside, in
command of the department, and called on the
people to resist it. General Burnside had him

arrested (4th of May), and ordered for trial by court-martial.   Mr. Vallandigham applied for a *habeas corpus*.   The court refused it, on the ground of public safety.   He was tried, found guilty, and sentenced to be placed in close confinement in a fortress.   The President directed him instead to be sent within the Confederate lines, not to return during the war.   He was at once turned loose accordingly into " Secessia." But he had been already puffed into a martyr by the Democrats.   A meeting was held at Albany (May 16), to which Governor Seymour of New York sent a letter, declaring that if the arrest was approved by the Government, it was " revolution," and " military despotism."   Resolutions denouncing arbitrary arrests and the suspension of the writ of *habeas corpus* were sent to the President.

Mr. Lincoln at once accepted the challenge. In a letter far too long to quote (13th of June), though it affords a most remarkable example of his powers of argument, he defended the whole course of his Government on the points on which

K

its conduct had been impugned. I will only extract one passage as to the arrest of Mr. Vallandigham himself. It was made, Mr. Lincoln wrote—" because he was labouring, with some effect, to prevent the raising of troops, to encourage desertions from the army, and to leave the rebellion without an adequate military force to suppress it. . . . . Must I shoot a simple-minded soldier-boy who deserts, while I must not touch a hair of a wily agitator who induces him to desert ? This is none the less injurious when effected by getting a father, or brother, or friend, into a public meeting, and there working upon his feelings till he is persuaded to write the soldier-boy that he is fighting in a bad cause, for a wicked Administration of a contemptible Government, too weak to arrest and punish him if he shall desert. I think that in such a case to silence the agitator and save the boy is not only constitutional, but withal a great mercy. . . . I can no more be persuaded that the Government can constitutionally take no strong measures in time of rebellion, because it can be shown that the same could not be lawfully taken in time of peace, than I can be persuaded that a particular drug is not good medicine for a sick man, because it can be shown not to be good food for a well one (*sic*). Nor am I able to appreciate the danger apprehended by the meeting, that the American people will, by means of military arrests during the rebellion, lose the right of public discussion, the liberty of speech and the press, the law of evidence, trial by jury, and *habeas corpus*, throughout the indefinite peaceful future which I trust lies before them, any more than I am able to believe that a man could contract so strong an appetite for emetics during temporary illness as to persist in feeding upon them during the remainder of his healthful life."

Adverting next to the title of "Democrats" claimed by the holders of the meeting, he said :—

"In this time of national peril, I would have preferred to meet you on a level one step higher than any party platform; because I am sure

that, from such more elevated position, we could
do better battle for the country we all love than
we possibly can from these lower ones, where,
from the force of habit, the prejudices of the
past, and selfish hopes of the future, we are sure
to expend much of our ingenuity and strength
in finding fault with and aiming blows at each
other."

But he reminded them that the General by
whose orders Mr. Vallandigham had been arrested, the judge who had refused the *habeas
corpus* on his behalf, were both Democrats; and
he recalled a well-known incident in the life of
General Jackson, the great hero of the Democratic party, who, not during the war with
England, but when peace was known to have
been concluded, though not officially announced,
not only maintained martial law, but arrested a
journalist who denounced it, then a lawyer who
sued out, and the judge who issued, a writ of
habeas corpus on his behalf, and another person
besides, and who, though fined for contempt of
Court, was eventually repaid both principal and

interest by Congress. With remarkable frank-
ness he however added :—

"And yet let me say that, in my own discretion, I do not know whether I would have
ordered the arrest of Mr. Vallandigham. . .
. . It gave me pain when I learned that Mr.
Vallandigham had been arrested—that is, I was
pained that there should have seemed to be a
necessity for arresting him. . . . . It will
afford me great pleasure to discharge him so
soon as I can, by any means, believe the public
safety will not suffer by it."

His arguments were, however thrown away
on the Democrats, who at their State convention
for the nomination of State officers in Ohio
(June 11th), made Mr. Vallandigham the candidate for Governor, by an almost unanimous
vote. The gravity of the Democratic opposition
at this juncture lay in this, that the Federal
territory was at this very moment invaded. On
the 9th of June it was discovered that Lee was
marching North-West through the Shenandoah
Valley. On the 13th, Lee's gallant lieutenant,

Ewell, drove Milroy disgracefully from Winchester. On the next day, the Confederate advance began crossing the Potomac, and the operation continued for a whole fortnight practically unimpeded, till the main body passed over on the 27th.* Meanwhile the Federal army, to which Lee had thus given the slip, was marching up from Fredericksburg, so as to cover Baltimore and Washington, Hooker being relieved in favour of the till now little known General Meade, who at once advanced into Pennsylvania, into which the Confederates had already penetrated. The two armies met before

---

* Mr. Lincoln's correspondence with General Hooker about this period contains many characteristic expressions, and seems to me to evince more military talent than he has usually been given credit for. On the 5th June he warns Hooker not to run any risk of being entangled on the Rappahannock—"like an ox jumped half over a fence and liable to be torn by dogs front and rear, without a fair chance to gore one way or to kick the other." On the 10th he warns Hooker not to "go south of the Rappahannock upon Lee's moving north of it. I think Lee's army, and not Richmond, is your true

Gettysburg; and the result of three days' fighting (July 1-3) was that the Confederates once more retreated, leaving 14,000 prisoners in the hands of the Federals,—the loss of the latter however exceeding 23,000 in all. To crown the glory of the 4th of July, 1863, Vicksburg surrendered on that day unconditionally to General Grant. The prisoners taken, who were at once paroled, were nearly 31,000 in number; besides 220 cannon, and 70,000 stand of small arms. Four days later, Port Hudson, which some time before had been unsuccessfully as-

objective point. If he comes towards the Upper Potomac, follow on his flank, and on the inside track, shortening your lines while he lengthens his. Fight him, too, when opportunity offers. If he stay where he is, fret him and fret him." On the 14th again :—"So far as we can make out here, the enemy have Milroy surrounded at Winchester, and Tyler at Martinsburg. If they could hold out a few days, could you help them ? If the head of Lee's army is at Martinsburg, and the tail of it on the flank road between Fredericksburg and Chancellorsville, the animal must be very slim somewhere ; could you not break him ?"

saulted by General Banks (the coloured troops fighting heroically in the action), surrendered also, with about 7,000 prisoners and 50 pieces of artillery. The Federals now controlled the whole course of the Mississippi; the Confederacy was cut in two. Rosecranz likewise had advanced from Murfreesboro', had turned the flank of Bragg's army at Tullahoma, and was driving him to the South-East, so as to force him back into Georgia. Against Charleston alone the Federal operations were but very partially successful; only securing Morris Island as a base of operations, and, in the unsuccessful assault of Fort Wagner, bringing out once more the bravery of the coloured troops.

This succession of triumphs caused general rejoicing in the North. At an early hour (10·30) on July 4, the President put forth a brief announcement of the successes at Gettysburg, for which " he especially desires that on this day He, whose will, not ours, should ever be done, be everywhere remembered and reverenced with profoundest gratitude." In the evening, after the news of the surrender of Vicksburg had come in, the President was serenaded, and replied as follows :—

"Fellow-citizens,—I am very glad indeed to see you to-night, and yet I will not say I thank you for this call; but I do most sincerely thank Almighty God for the occasion on which you have called. How long ago is it? eighty-odd years since, on the 4th of July, for the first time in the history of the world, a nation, by its representatives, assembled and declared as a self-evident truth, that all men are created equal. That was the birthday of the United States of America. Since then the Fourth of July has had several very peculiar recognitions. The two men most distinguished in the framing and support of the Declaration were Thomas Jefferson and John Adams—the one having penned it and the other sustained it the most forcibly in debate—the only two of the fifty-five who signed it, and were elected Presidents of the United States. Precisely fifty years after they put their hands to the paper, it pleased Almighty God to take both from this stage of action. . . . Another President, five years after, was called from this stage of existence on the same day and month of the year; and now, on this last Fourth of July just passed, when we have a gigantic rebellion, at the bottom of which is an effort to overthrow the principle that all men were created equal, we have the surrender of a most powerful position and army on that very day. And not only so, but in a succession of battles in Pennsylvania, near to us, so rapidly fought that they might be called one great battle, on the 1st, 2nd, and 3rd of the month of July, and on the 4th the cohorts of those who opposed the Declaration that all men are created equal ' turned tail ' and ran. . . . I would like to speak in terms of praise due to the many brave officers and soldiers who have fought in the cause of the Union and liberties of their country from the beginning of the war. These are trying occasions, not only in success, but for the want of success. I dislike to mention the name of one single officer, lest I might do wrong to those I might forget."

But whilst thus tender to the sensitiveness of the "many brave," there was one brave man to whom the President shortly after (July 13) wrote this beautiful letter:—

"Major-General Grant:

"My dear General,—I do not remember that you and I ever met personally. I write this now as a grateful acknowledgment for the almost inestimable service you have done the country. I write to say one word further. When you first reached the vicinity of Vicksburg, I thought you should do what you finally did—march the troops across the neck, run the batteries with the transports, and thus go below; and I never had any faith, except a general hope that you knew better than I, that the Yazoo Pass expedition, and the like, could succeed. When you got below, and took Port Gibson, Grand Gulf, and vicinity, I thought you should go down the river and join General

Banks; and when you turned northward, east of the Big Black, I feared it was a mistake. I now wish to make the personal acknowledgment that you were right and I was wrong."

A proclamation for a national thanksgiving (July 15) must also be quoted:—

" It has pleased Almighty God to hearken to the supplications and prayers of an afflicted people, and to vouchsafe to the army and the navy of the United States, on the land and on the sea, victories so signal and so effective as to furnish reasonable grounds for augmented confidence that the union of these States will be maintained, their constitution preserved, and their peace and prosperity permanently secured; but those victories have been attended not without sacrifice of life, limb, and liberty, incurred by brave, patriotic, and loyal citizens. Domestic affliction, in every part of the country, follows in the train of these fearful bereavements. It is meet and right to recognise and confess the presence of the Almighty Father, and the power of His hand, equally in these triumphs and these sorrows.

" Now, therefore, be it known that I do set apart Thursday, the 6th day of August next, to be observed as a day for National Thanksgiving, praise, and prayer; and I invite the people of the United States to assemble on that occasion in their customary places of worship, and, in the form approved by their own conscience, render the homage due to the Divine Majesty for the wonderful things He has done in the nation's behalf, and invoke the influence of His Holy Spirit, to subdue the anger which has produced, and so long sustained, a needless and cruel rebellion ; to change the hearts of the insurgents; to guide the counsels of the Government with wisdom adequate to so great a national emergency; and to visit with tender care and consolation, throughout the length and breadth of our land, all those who, through the vicissitudes of marches, voyages, battles, and sieges, have been brought to suffer in mind, body, or estate; and, finally, to lead the whole nation, through paths of repentance and submission to the Divine will, back to the perfect enjoyment of union and fraternal peace."

Do not utterances like these make one feel that in their highest earthly, as in their heavenly embodiment, the king and the priest are one?

The battle of Gettysburg, the surrender of Vicksburg and Port Hudson, and the driving of Bragg through Tennessee, must be looked upon as forming together the turning-point of the war. It was now seen that, whilst the Federals could successfully invade and occupy the South, the Confederates could not successfully invade and occupy the North. Antietam had been only a check to them; but at Gettysburg, the Federal army of the Potomac, tried by so many disasters, had won its first victory, and that under a commander just installed in the chief command. The fallacious prestige which had surrounded M'Clellan's name was henceforth dispelled. The country could be saved without him.

Yet it was in the very flush of victory, both

East and West, that the most serious internal disturbances broke out. On the 13th July, the carrying out of the Conscription Act was resisted in New York, and for four days mob-law ruled supreme in the great city. The officers connected with the draft, the administration, the coloured race, were alike objects of the popular fury. Negroes were beaten to death, hung, mutilated ; a coloured orphan asylum was sacked and set on fire. The State authorities, Democrats, stood by, almost passive. The Roman Catholic Archbishop Hughes coaxed and blarneyed the rioters (almost all Irishmen). Governor Seymour asked the postponement of the draft, *i.e.* that the mob should be yielded to. The President refused, and on the 19th August it was resumed, and carried out without opposition. The New York riots bore exactly the opposite result to what the plotters of them intended. They raised the indignation of the country, heightened the anti-slavery feeling, and crushed the Democrats. In Ohio, Mr. Vallandigham was defeated for the governorship by a

majority of nearly 100,000 ; New York was won
by the Republicans ; in short, every State except
New Jersey recorded by its votes its approval of
the Government policy.   To this electoral
campaign belongs a memorable letter of Mr.
Lincoln's (August 26), to an invitation from the
Republican State Committee of Illinois to attend
a State convention at Springfield. " Uncon-
ditional Union men," they were yet dissatisfied
with the President " about the negro," and dis-
liked his emancipation proclamation.   After
various arguments in its defence, the President
said :—

" You say you will not fight to free negroes.
Some of them seem willing to fight for you ; but
no matter.   Fight you, then, exclusively to save
the Union. . . .   Whenever you shall have
conquered all resistance to the Union, if I shall
urge you to continue fighting, it will be an apt
time then for you to declare you will not fight to
free negroes.   I thought that in your struggle
for the Union, to whatever extent the negroes
should cease helping the enemy, to that extent

it weakened the enemy in his resistance to you.
Do you think differently ? I thought that whatever negroes can be got to do as soldiers, leaves
just so much less for white soldiers to do in saving
the Union.   Does it appear otherwise to you ?
But negroes, like other people, act upon motives.
Why should they do anything for us, if we will
do nothing for them ?   If they stake their lives
for us, they must be prompted by the strongest
motive, even the promise of freedom.   *And
the promise, being made, must be kept.*"

Next comes a rapid sketch of the " bettering
of the signs," in that homely but picturesque
language in which Mr. Lincoln excelled, containing the odd image of " Uncle Sam's web feet"
making their tracks " wherever the ground was
a little damp :"—

" The Father of waters " [*i. e.* the Mississippi],
" again goes unvexed to the sea. Thanks to the
great North-West for it, and yet not wholly to
them.   Three hundred miles up they met New
England, Empire " [New York], " Keystone "
[Pennsylvania], "and" [New] "Jersey, hewing

L

their way right and left.   The sunny South, too, in more colours than one, also lent a helping hand.   On the spot, their part of history was jotted down in black and white.   The job was a great national one, and let none be slighted who took an honourable part in it.   And while those who have cleared the great river may well be proud, even that is not all.   It is hard to say that anything has been more bravely and well done than at Antietam, Murfreesborough, Gettysburg, and on many fields of less note. Nor must Uncle Sam's web feet be forgotten. At all the watery margins they have been present, not only on the deep sea, the broad bay, and the rapid river, but also up the narrow, muddy bayou, and wherever the ground was a little damp, they have been and made their tracks. Thanks to all. For the great Republic— for the principle it lives by and keeps alive—for man's future—thanks to all."

In graver strain he concluded : —" Peace does not appear so distant as it did. I hope it will come soon, and come to stay : and so come

as to be worth the keeping in all future time.
It will then have been proved that among free
men there can be no successful appeal from the
ballot to the bullet, and that they who take
such appeal are sure to lose their case and pay
the cost.   And there will be some black men
who can remember that, with silent tongue, and
clenched teeth, and steady eye, and well-poised
bayonet, they have helped mankind on to this
great consummation ; while I fear there will be
some white ones unable to forget that with
malignant heart and deceitful speech they have
striven to hinder it.   Still, let us not be over
sanguine of a speedy, final triumph.   Let us be
quite sober.   Let us diligently apply the means,
never doubting that a just God, in His own good
time, will give us the rightful result."

The careless yet most genuine eloquence of
passages such as the last is not easily to be
surpassed.

The Autumn of 1863 saw one serious Federal
reverse.   General Rosecranz had crowned his
already great military reputation by his pursuit

of General Bragg through South Eastern Tennessee, till he had at last compelled him (9th September) to evacuate the Confederate stronghold of Chattanooga—key to all the lines of communication through what has been termed "a great mountain labyrinth." Simultaneously with this movement, General Burnside advanced through Eastern Tennessee, till now unwillingly subject to Confederate rule, and entered, amidst the acclamations of the inhabitants, its chief city, Knoxville. But whether or not rendered overconfident by success, Rosecranz received, ten days later, at Chickamauga (19th September), a terrible defeat from Bragg, reinforced by Longstreet, Lee's best lieutenant, losing upwards of 16,000 men in killed and wounded, and missing. Only one portion of Rosecranz's army, that under Thomas, repelled successfully all attacks, and no doubt saved Chattanooga, where, however, the Federals found themselves shut up with very scant supplies; Longstreet meanwhile being sent off against Burnside at Knoxville. Rosecranz was at once replaced by

Grant in command of the Federal army of the Tennessee; whilst Sherman, with a portion of that of the Mississippi, was hurried on to reinforce him.

Under these somewhat gloomy circumstances President Lincoln had to speak (19th November, 1863), on the dedication of a national burying-ground on the field of Gettysburg. His speech on this occasion appears to me simply one of the noblest extant specimens of human eloquence :*—

" Fourscore and seven years ago our fathers brought forth upon this continent a new nation, conceived in liberty, and dedicated to the proposition that all men are created equal. Now we are engaged in a great civil war, testing whether that nation, or any nation so conceived and so dedicated, can long endure. We are met

---

* "Je ne crois pas que l'éloquence moderne ait jamais rien produit de plus élevé que le discours prononcé par lui" (*i. e.* by President Lincoln) "sur la tombe des soldats morts à Gettysburg," (M. E. Duƒergier de Hauranne, "Revue des Deux Mondes," for Jan. 15, 1866, p. 489).

Of the old Jansenist family, from which, in earlier times, came the Abbé de St. Cyran, who, with Cornelius Jansen, founded the Jansenists

on a great battle-field of that war. We have come to dedicate a portion of that field as a final resting-place for those who here gave their lives that that nation might live. It is altogether fitting and proper that we should do this. But in a larger sense we cannot dedicate, we cannot consecrate, we cannot hallow, this ground. The brave men, living and dead, who struggled here, have consecrated it far above our power to add or detract. The world will little note, nor long remember, what we say here ; but it can never forget what they did here. It is for us, the living, rather to be dedicated here to the unfinished work which they who fought here have thus far so nobly advanced. It is rather for us to be here dedicated to the great task remaining before us, that from these honoured dead we take increased devotion to that cause for which they gave the last full measure of devotion ; that we here highly resolve that these dead shall not have died in vain ; that this nation, under God, shall have a new birth of freedom, and that government of the people, by the people, and for the people, shall not perish from the earth."

The reverse of Chickamauga might have added solemnity to the President's words. The words themselves were heralds of triumph. Grant had taken in hand the beaten army, adding to it his own veterans. On the 23rd, he moved out to attack Bragg, and on the 25th, in great measure through Sherman's desperate valour, the Confederates were driven from their strong positions, and pursued by Thomas and Hooker into Georgia, whilst Granger and Sherman were sent to relieve Burnside at Knoxville. But already Longstreet had been beaten off in an assault; he now raised the siege, but effected a masterly retreat into Virginia. The President called for another thanksgiving (7th of December.)

I need not dwell upon Mr. Lincoln's third Annual Message (9th of December, 1863). Appended to it is, however, a remarkable proclamation (8th December,) containing his scheme for reconstruction of the Union. With certain exceptions, a full amnesty was tendered to all who should take an oath of loyalty to the United

States, binding them to "abide by and faithfully
support all acts of Congress passed during the
existing rebellion with reference to slaves, so
long and so far as not repealed, modified, or
held void by Congress, or by decision of the
Supreme Court;" also "all proclamations of the
President made during the existing rebellion
having reference to slaves, so long and so far as
not modified or declared void by decision of
the Supreme Court." The exceptions comprised
amongst others, "all who have engaged in any
way in treating coloured persons, or white
persons in charge of such," being in the service
of the United States, " otherwise than lawfully
as prisoners of war,"—the Confederate authorities having proclaimed that all coloured soldiers
of the United States, or their officers, were to
receive no quarter. Mr. Lincoln then provided
that any number of persons, not less than one-
tenth in number of the votes cast in the ten
States of the original secession in 1860, having
taken and kept the oath of loyalty, and being
qualified voters under their respective State laws

before secession, might re-establish a State Government in conformity with the oath ; adding that any provision to be adopted by such State government in relation to the freed people of such State, which should " recognise and declare their permanent freedom, provide for their education," and might " yet be consistent, as a temporary arrangement, with their present condition as a labouring, landless, and homeless class," would " not be objected to by the National Executive."

Among the measures of Congress passed this session, I will only mention the establishment of a " Bureau of Freedmen's Affairs," to determine all questions relating to the coloured people, and regulate their employment and proper treatment. A proposed amendment of the constitution abolishing slavery absolutely was adopted by the Senate, and by a majority of the House of Representatives, but did not obtain in the latter the two-thirds vote required by the Constitution.

The military operations of the early part of

1864 were unsuccessful or unimportant. An
expedition into the heart of Florida, one of the
main sources of supply to the Confederates, led
to the Federal defeat of Olustee (20th February,
1864). Sherman marched Eastward from Vicksburg (3rd February), and reached Meridian,
almost on the border of Alabama ; but a cavalry
force from Memphis having failed to join him,
he retreated. A dashing cavalry raid by General
Kilpatrick, in the rear of Lee's army, led the
Federals through the outer line of the fortifications of Richmond, and up to the second line,
two and a half miles from the city (1st March,
1864) ; but part of the force under Colonel
Dahlgren was defeated and captured, himself
killed, and the rest withdrew, having thus failed
in the attempt to surprise Richmond or deliver
the Federal prisoners (whose maltreatment by
the Confederate authorities had created deep
indignation throughout the North). Lastly, a
serious disaster befel the Federals in the West,
on an advance up the valley of the Red River,
one of the great westerly affluents of the Mis-

sissippi (March); General Banks being completely defeated by General Kirby Smith, and having to fall back with a loss of 16,000 men, whilst a flotilla of gunboats was only saved by engineering ingenuity. Banks was speedily relieved of his command. Lastly, Fort Pillow on the Mississippi was captured by Forrest's Confederates, and a frightful massacre of the Federal soldiers (chiefly coloured) perpetrated after their surrender (12th April); and a few days later the capture by the Confederates of Plymouth (North Carolina), was followed by a similar massacre on a smaller scale (April 20th). Still, most of these movements had for effect to cut up Confederate railway lines, destroy their supplies, and show the Federal flag and uniform in quarters where they had not been seen since the secession. Kilpatrick's raid in particular (coupled with a wonderful 500 miles' ride during the previous year of Colonel Grierson and his men, from Memphis to New Orleans, through a tract of country still almost entirely in Confederate hands), helped to raise the confidence of the Federal cavalry, at first greatly outshone by the Confederate, under its dashing leader, J. E. B. (familiarly called Jeb) Stuart.

Among the public utterances of the President at this period, may be noted his reply (21st March, 1864) to an address from the " Working Men's Association of New York," requesting permission to enrol him an honorary member of the association. The association, he said, comprehended " that the existing rebellion means more and tends to do more than the perpetuation of African slavery—that it is, in fact, a war upon the rights of all working people.

" None are so deeply interested to resist the present rebellion as the working people. Let them beware of prejudices, working division and hostility among themselves. The most notable feature of a disturbance in your city last summer, was the hanging of some working people by some other working people. It should never be so. The strongest bond of human sympathy, outside of the family relation, should be one uniting all working people of all nations, and tongues, and kindreds. Nor should this lead to a war upon property, or the owners of property. Property is the fruit of labour ; property is desirable ; is a positive good in the world. That some should be rich shows that others may become rich, and hence is just encouragement to industry and enterprise. Let not him who is houseless pull down the house of another ; but let him labour diligently and build one for himself, thus by example assuring that his shall be safe from violence when built."

It need hardly be pointed out how, in alluding to the New York riots of the previous year, and to the outrages then committed against the coloured men, Mr. Lincoln deliberately ignores the distinction of colour, when speaking of " the hanging of some working people by other working people."

Nor can I overlook a letter (4th April) written for the purpose of putting on record his previous verbal reply to a deputation from Kentucky on the subject of the draft. After saying, " I am naturally anti-slavery. If slavery is not wrong, nothing is wrong. I cannot remember when I did not so think and feel," he explained the causes which had prevented him as President from acting on this feeling until such time as, through the failure of his appeals for compensated emancipation, he felt himself " driven to the alternative of either surrendering the Union, and with it the Constitution, or of laying strong hold upon the coloured element." He chose the latter, not " entirely confident" in so doing of greater gain than loss. But

" More than a year of trial now shows no loss by it in our foreign relations, none in our home popular sentiment, none in our white military force, no loss by it anyhow or anywhere. On the contrary, it shows a gain of quite 130,000 soldiers, sailors and labourers. . . . We have the men, and we could not have had them without the measure. . . . In telling this tale, I attempt no compliment to my own sagacity. I claim not to have controlled events, but confess plainly that events have controlled me. Now, at the end of three years' struggle, the nation's condition is not what either party, or any man, devised or expected. . . . If God now wills the removal of a great wrong, and wills also that we of the North, as well as you of the South, shall pay fairly for our complicity in that wrong, impartial history will find therein new causes to attest and revere the justice and goodness of God."

An extract must also be given from a speech of Mr. Lincoln's about this period (18th of April), delivered at Baltimore, Maryland, at the opening of a fair for the benefit of the Sanitary Commission :—

" The world has never had a good definition of the word liberty, and the American people just now are much in want of one. We all declare for liberty ; but in using the same *word* we do not all mean the same *thing*. With some the word liberty may mean for each man to do as he pleases with himself, and the product of his labour ; while with others the same word may mean for some men to do as they please with other men, and the product of other men's labour.　Here are two, not only different, but incompatible things, called by the same name, liberty.　And it follows that each of the things is, by the respective parties, called by two different and incompatible names—liberty and tyranny.　The shepherd drives the wolf from the sheep's throat, for which the sheep thanks the shepherd as a *liberator*, while the wolf denounces him for the same act, as the destroyer of liberty, especially as the sheep was a black one.　Plainly, the sheep and the wolf are not agreed upon a definition of word liberty. . . . Hence we behold the process by which thousands are daily passing from under the yoke of bondage, hailed by some as the advance of liberty, and bewailed by others as the destruction of all liberty."

Much of the speech is devoted to an endeavour to allay the public indignation, just now greatly excited by the news of the late massacre in cold blood (not the first by the Confederates during the war), at Fort Pillow, the cry being loud for retaliation against the Confederate prisoners in

Federal hands, under the provisions of a general order to this effect, issued 30th July, 1863 ; but in vain. Yet although the Federal Government still abstained from taking the life of one Confederate prisoner in retaliation for the slaughter of its coloured soldiers, it was making a far more painful sacrifice to their rights. For many long months, whilst the Federal prisoners were starving and rotting at the South, the Confederate Government professed its willingness to exchange all the white prisoners in its hands, and latterly even the negroes, natives of the North, who had enlisted ; provided only it was allowed to do its will on those from the Confederate States taken with arms in their hands. Piteous appeals reached the North from the white prisoners themselves at Charleston. The Democrats made capital of their sufferings to declaim against the inhumanity of the Government. Nobly inflexible the Federal Cabinet remained, till at last (I anticipate on events to dispose of this matter) an agreement to exchange man for man was accepted by the Confederate

M

authorities; but before it could be entirely carried
out, the final success of the Federal arms rendered it useless by setting free the prisoners
in the South.*

The spring campaigns of 1864 were now at
hand.   The chief command of all the United

* I insert here slightly out of chronological order
an extract from a speech made on a similar occasion,
at a Sanitary Fair in Philadelphia (June 1864) :—

" War at the best is terrible, and this of ours, in its
magnitude and duration, is one of the most terrible the
world has ever known.   It has deranged business totally
in many places, and perhaps in all.   It has destroyed
property, destroyed life, and ruined homes.   It has produced a national debt and a degree of taxation unpre-
cedented in the history of the country.   It has caused
mourning among us until the heavens may almost be said
to be hung in black ;—and yet it continues.   It has had
accompaniments not before known in the history of the
world ; I mean the Sanitary and Christian Commission,
with their labours for the relief of the soldiers, and the
Volunteer refreshment saloons, understood better by
those who hear me than by myself ; and these fairs, first
begun at Chicago, and next held in Boston, Cincinnati,
and other cities. . . . . From the fair and tender hand
of woman is much, very much done for the soldier,
continually reminding him of the care and thought for

States armies had been vested in General Grant. The President addressed to him the following letter (April 30) :—

" Lieut.-General Grant :

" Not expecting to seeing you before the spring campaign opens, I wish to express in this way my entire satisfaction with what you have done up to this time, so far as I understand it.

" The particulars of your plans I neither know nor seek to know. You are vigilant and self-reliant ; and, pleased with this, I wish not to obtrude any restraints and constraints upon you. While I am very anxious that any great disaster or capture of our men in great numbers shall be avoided, I know that these points are less likely to escape your atten-

him at home. The knowledge that he is not forgotten is grateful to his heart. Another view of these institutions is worthy of thought. They are voluntary contributions, giving proof that the national resources are not at all exhausted, and that the national patriotism will sustain us through all."

tion than they would be mine. If there be anything wanting which is within my power to give, do not fail to let me know it.

" And now, with a brave army and a just cause, may God sustain you ! " *

---

* General Grant's reply (May 1), deserves to be inserted, were it only by way of contrast to the querulousness of a M'Clellan :—

" The President :

" Your very kind letter of yesterday is just received. The confidence you express for the future, and satisfaction for the past, in my military administration, is acknowledged with pride. It will be my earnest endeavour that you and the country shall not be disappointed. From my first entrance into the volunteer service of the country to the present day, I have never had cause of complaint, have never expressed or implied a complaint against the Administration, or the Secretary of War, for throwing any embarrassment in the way of my vigorously prosecuting what appeared to be my duty.

" Indeed, since the promotion which placed me in command of all the armies, and in view of the great responsibility and importance of success, I have been astonished at the readiness with which every thing asked for has been yielded, without even an explanation being asked. Should my success be less than I deserve and expect, the least I can say is, the fault is not with you."

Grant's plan was simply to concentrate almost all the United States' forces into two great armies, which should strike simultaneous blows North and South.* Accordingly, on the 5th May commenced the final campaigns of the war, consisting, the one of a renewed march of the army of the Potomac upon Richmond, under Grant and Meade, the other of Sherman's successive advances from Chattanooga toward the Atlantic coast, and from thence again Northwards—campaigns on the details of which I cannot dwell, although each is of surpassing interest. In Virginia a veteran and consummate general, Robert Lee, operating, as

At last the President and his Commander-in-Chief could understand one another.

* Till now, as General Grant tells us in his report on the operations of the United States' armies since his appointment to the chief command (dated July 25, 1865, but only published in December)—a most interesting and remarkable contribution to military literature—the armies in the East and West had "acted independently and without concert, like a balky *(sic)* team, no two ever pulling together."

he indeed has almost always done throughout the war, not only within his own territory, but upon carefully studied, carefully fortified ground, every inch of which almost is personally familiar to him, and leading an army, small comparatively in numbers, but used to victory, finds himself confronted by a much younger chief, Ulysses Grant; new indeed to the country, but who has fought his way through a thousand miles of hostile soil, and has won almost each successive victory on fresh ground; new to the oft-defeated army he commands, but whose most recent achievement has been to lead beaten troops to victory. Each possesses the full confidence of his men; Lee's name, never yet but once associated with absolute defeat, is a guarantee that all that military skill can do will be done to secure success; Grant's tender care for the soldier at any but the hour of battle enables him, when that hour has struck, to demand from his troops the utmost sacrifices;*

* General Grant was determined, he tells us in his report, "to hammer continuously against the armed force

whilst by his side the modest victor of Gettysburg, Meade, too diffident to bear the responsibility of directing a campaign, is yet ready to
carry out with unflinching zeal and unerring
intelligence the plans of his younger and bolder
chief. Between these foemen, each full worthy
of the other's steel, the scales to many seem long
to tremble equal. Flinging himself across the
Rapidan before his enemy can oppose him,
Grant enters that terrible " wilderness," — a
broken, wooded country, where artillery cannot
manœuvre, where every knoll and clump aud
patch of scrub may hide a murderous ambuscade,
in which Hooker before him lost his head, and
those many thousands whose whited skeletons
still cumber the ground. He is met here by
the enemy, confident of winning new triumphs.
But where Hooker had only fought and struggled away, Grant fights and struggles through.

of the enemy and his resources, until by mere attrition,
if in no other way, there should no nothing left to him"
but submission " to the Constitution and laws of the
land."

The slaughter is immense; but on the third
day (5th—7th May), Lee falls back on his
second line of defence.   Meanwhile, from Fortress Monroe, General Butler has succeeded in
occupying Bermuda Hundred, an important
point on the James River, thus giving a foothold
to the East of Richmond.*   By a series of flank
marches, Grant forces Lee, though still at the
cost of fearful slaughter, step by step, back
upon Richmond, yet without being able to
reach the oft-approached goal, until at last
(June 12th), by a movement less expected than
any, he swings round to the South, and takes
up that position before Petersburg, which he is
to hold during so many months.   Washington
lies indeed thereby uncovered, and the failure of
General Hunter's operations in North-Western

* Butler's subsequent operations were not successful.
" He was forced back or drew back," General Grant
drily says, into his entrenchments, between the forks of
two rivers, where his army, "though in a position of
great security, was as completely shut off from further
operations against Richmond as if it had been in a bottle
strongly corked."

Virginia soon calls the Confederates over the Potomac. On the 7th July the President has to issue a proclamation, calling for 12,000 men from each of the two States of Pennsylvania and New York, and stating that a Confederate force of from 15,000 to 20,000 has invaded Maryland, taken Martinsburg and Harper's Ferry, and threatens other points. In Kentucky, too, John Morgan has made one of his daring inroads, and has nearly reached the Ohio, so that martial law and the suspension of the *habeas corpus* have to be proclaimed in Kentucky (5th July), whilst a day of humiliation is also appointed (7th July), the President exhorting the people to pray for the early suppression of the rebellion, before the Southern people are utterly destroyed. But their invasion of Maryland and Pennsylvania eventually proves a mere raiding expedition to procure supplies, —thus both showing the dearth already existing in Confederate Virginia, and provoking further Federal ravages; and none of these various attempts avail to make Grant shift his position, or release his gripe on the neck of the Southern capital.

Sherman, on his part, was performing the first, and only really contested one, of his three great marches, that from Chattanooga to Atlanta. His army was numerous,—100,000 men, with 250 pieces of artillery; but the country was most difficult, and he had in front of him, at the head of forces perhaps not more than half his own, but superior in cavalry, a skilful and wary adversary, Joseph Johnstone, who on one occasion · (Sherman's unsuccessful attack at Kenesaw, June 27), inflicted on him a loss of 2500 men. But by means of that strategy which earned him, from his soldiers, the nickname of "Old Pothook," throwing always a portion of his forces round his adversary's position to some point in the rear, Sherman compelled Johnstone to evacuate one strong position after the other, till at last, when nearly within reach of Atlanta, his success was hastened through Johnstone's supersession (17th July) by the gallant but shallow-headed

Hood, who took the offensive, got several times beaten, and soon saw Sherman in Atlanta, and himself out of it (2nd September).

Meanwhile another momentous campaign was proceeding. The four years' term of office of Mr. Lincoln, as President, would expire in March, 1865. The new Presidential election would take place in November. Who was to be the next President? The Democrats put forward General M'Clellan; the ultra-Abolitionists, General Fremont (who, however, resigned his candidateship before the election).* But the "National Union" Convention at Baltimore (June 8th), unanimously adopted Abraham Lincoln and Andrew Johnson as candidates for the Presidency and Vice-Presidency, on a "platform," recommending an amendment of the constitution, to "terminate and for ever prohibit the existence of slavery within the limits of the jurisdiction of the United States;" embodying a hearty approval

* General Grant peremptorily refused to become a candidate.

of the emancipation proclamation, of the military employment of former slaves; and recognising the duty of affording protection to all persons, of whatever colour, employed in the national armies. Mr. Lincoln accepted the nomination, provisionally at first (June 9), then formally (June 27). But his most characteristic expression of feeling on the occasion was in reply to a congratulatory address, from the "National Union League" (June 9), when his last words were :—

" I have not permitted myself, gentlemen, to conclude that I am the best man in the country; but I am reminded in this connection of a story of an old Dutch farmer, who remarked to a companion once that 'it was not best to swap horses when crossing a stream.'"

The same evening he said, in answer to a serenade (which he said was "the hardest of all speeches I have to answer"):—

" What we want still more than Baltimore conventions, or Presidential elections, is success under General Grant. I propose that you con-

stantly bear in mind that the support you owe
to the brave officers and soldiers in the field is
of the very first importance, and we should,
therefore, bend all our energies to that point."*

---

* It is a singular circumstance that Mr. Lincoln learnt
the nomination of Mr. Johnson as Vice-President, before
learning his own nomination. He was reminded by this
incident of one connected with his original nomination
at Chicago, which he thus related the same day to Mr.
Carpenter and to Mr. John Hay, his assistant private
secretary :—

"In the afternoon of the day, returning home from
down town, I went up-stairs to Mrs. Lincoln's sitting-
room. Feeling somewhat tired, I lay down upon a
couch in the room, directly opposite a bureau, upon
which was a looking-glass. As I reclined, my eye fell
upon the glass, and I saw distinctly two images of myself, exactly alike, except that one was a little paler than
the other. I arose and lay down again with the same
result. It made me quite uncomfortable for a few mo-
ments ; but some friends coming in, the matter passed
out of my mind. The next day, while walking in the
street, I was suddenly reminded of the circumstance, and
the disagreeable sensation produced by it returned. I
had never seen anything of the kind before, and did not
know what to make of it. I determined to go home
and place myself in the same position ; and, if the same

Mr. Lincoln's nomination gave great strength to the Republican, or as it may now be called, the National party, and weakened to a corresponding extent whatever hopes the Confederates might have built on Northern dissensions. It was accordingly followed, not long after, by an attempt at negotiation. Three semi-official Confederate Commissioners applied for a safe-conduct to Washington, there to treat of peace. There was a trap concealed in the offer, which deceived even old Republican Abolitionists. If the President consented to treat, without any stipulation as to the restoration of the Union, he forfeited all title to support as a Union candidate. If he

effect was produced, I would make up my mind that it was the natural result of some principle of refraction or optics which I did not understand, and dismiss it. I tried the experiment with the same result; and, as I had said to myself, accounting for it on some principle unknown to me, it ceased to trouble me."

But the God who works *through* the laws of nature might surely give a sign to one of His chosen servants, even through the operation of a principle in optics.

did so without any stipulation as to the abolition of slavery, he forfeited all title to support
from the Abolitionists and the coloured people.
And if the self-proposed Commissioners were
not accredited by an authority controlling the
war-power, the only result of admitting them
might be to introduce into the capital, at a time
of political crisis, a set of intriguers who would
foment civil discord, and deaden military operations by negotiations which would lead to
nothing. Mr. Lincoln saw through the plot,
and baffled it by a safe-conduct (July 18th)
combining in a marvellous manner the harmless-
ness of the dove with the wisdom of the serpent:

" To whom it may concern :—Any proposition which embraces the restoration of peace,
the integrity of the whole Union, and the abandonment of slavery, and which comes by and
with an authority that can control the armies
now at war against the United States, will be
received and considered by the Executive
Government of the United States, and will be
met by liberal terms on substantial and collateral

points, and the bearer or bearers thereof shall have safe conduct both ways."

Utterly discomfited, the plotters went their way, writing indignant letters to the newspapers.* The Democratic party did .not, however, abandon the attempt to carry M'Clellan's election. There was great depression in the public mind. The Confederates were raiding again in Maryland and Pennsylvania, burning in the latter State the town of Chambersburg (30th July), and only recrossing the Potomac on the 7th August. Grant met with a severe repulse in an assault on Petersburg (July 30), and only gained some decided advantage by the occupation of the Weldon Railroad, one of Lee's channels of supply (17th August). A call by Mr. Lincoln for 500,000 men (July 18th)

* I am expressing here what I believe to be the calm judgment of an on-looker on the substantial result of the proceedings. At the same time, it appears certain that, through the suppression by. an unwise friend of certain material facts, to which Mr. Lincoln submitted in silence, his reputation suffered by the intrigue for the time. See Mr. Raymond's work, pp. 571—590.

showed his sense of the gravity of the crisis. Friends sought to dissuade him from the act, lest he should damage his electioneering prospects. "As to my re-election," he replied, "it matters not. We must have the men. If I go down, I intend to go, like the '*Cumberland*,'* with my colours flying."† He looked haggard

* A wooden frigate sunk by the Confederate iron-clad *Merrimac* in Hampton Roads.

† With the same disdain of personal consequences in calling upon a weary people for fresh sacrifices, Mr. Lincoln had concluded his speech at the Philadelphia Sanitary Fair in June (see ante, p. 162, *n.*), by an appeal for men :—

"It is a pertinent question, When is this war to end? I do not wish to name a day when it will end, lest the end should not come at the given time. We accepted this war, and did not begin it. We accepted it for an object, and when that object is accomplished, the war will end, *and I hope to God it will never end until that object is accomplished.* We are going through with our task, so far as I am concerned, if it takes us three years longer. . . . If I discover that General Grant may be greatly facilitated in the capture of Richmond, by rapidly pouring in to him a large number of armed men at the briefest notice, will you go? Will you march on with him? (Cries of 'Yes, yes.') Then I shall call upon you when it is necessary."

N

and careworn, and was told it was from over-
work. " I can't work less," he answered, "but
it isn't that—work never troubled me. Personally I care nothing about a re-election, but
if our divisions defeat us, I fear for the country."
He did not indeed despair of the result. " But I
may never live to see it. I feel a presentiment
that I shall not outlast the rebellion. When it
is over, my work will be done."

One main grievance against Mr. Lincoln was
the employment of negro soldiers. In a conversation with Judge Mills, of Wisconsin, the
latter reports the President to have thus expressed himself on the subject :—

"There have been men base enough to propose to me to return to slavery the black war-
riors of Port Hudson and Olustee, and thus win
the respect of the masters they fought. Should
I do so, I should deserve to be damned in time
and eternity. Come what will, I will keep my
faith with friend and foe. My enemies pretend
I am now carrying on this war for the sole purpose of abolition. So long as I am President,
it shall be carried on for the sole purpose of

restoring the Union. But no human power can subdue this rebellion without the use of the emancipation policy. Freedom has given us 200,000 men, raised on Southern soil. It will give us more yet. . . . Let my enemies prove to the country that the destruction of slavery is not necessary to the restoration of the Union. I will abide the issue."

But by the autumn the gloom began to pass away. The month of September, besides witnessing severe fighting in the neighbourhood of Petersburg, where Grant was establishing his own position, and gradually obtaining control of, or destroying various railway lines by which Richmond communicates with the South, saw the rise into prominence of a young commander hitherto known only as a cavalry leader, by various dashing raids through Virginia. Placed in command of the general Federal forces in North-Western Virginia, the scene of so many of "Stonewall" Jackson's exploits, Sheridan showed that the valley of the Shenandoah was, in turn, to witness Federal successes; and in a couple of brilliant battles (September 19, 23) defeated and drove before him the Confederate General Early, taking from him almost all his artillery. Undaunted by defeat, Early took advantage of a temporary absence of Sheridan, and of a dense fog, to attack his army before daylight (October 19th), driving it in confusion four miles before him. The news reached Sheridan, fortunately not very far distant, hastening to his army. Without bringing with him so much as a company to reinforce it, he yet brought victory with his presence; attacked Early that afternoon with his routed troops, and routed him, retaking all captured guns, and as many besides, with some 1,600 prisoners. Washington was never henceforth seriously threatened, although the guerrilla chief, Mosby, might still carry on small raids and skirmishes on its neighbouring railway lines. Mr. Lincoln issued a Thanksgiving Proclamation (October 20th), and wrote the following letter to General Sheridan (October 22nd):—

" With great pleasure I tender to you, and to

your brave army, the thanks of the nation, and my own personal admiration and gratitude for the month's operations in the Shenandoah Valley, and especially for the splendid work of October 19th."

Another public expression of thanks on the part of the President should also be recorded. With our European notions of warfare, we can hardly conceive without disgust of regiments leaving the front in the midst of a war, because their time is out. The feeling is far otherwise where the great bulk of an army are only citizens engaging themselves for short periods, and trying to apportion their time as well as possible between military and civil necessities. There is no shame then in withdrawing, whilst others take the place of those departing, on similar conditions. Accordingly, we find Mr. Lincoln more than once addressing such homeward bound regiments, without a tinge of disapproval, e.g., (October) :

" Soldiers,—I suppose you are going home to see your families and friends. For the services you have done in this great struggle in which we are engaged, I present you sincere thanks for myself and the country. I almost always feel inclined, when I say anything to soldiers, to impress upon them, in a few brief remarks, the importance of success in this contest. It is not merely for the day, but for all time to come, that we should perpetuate for our children's children that great and free government which we have enjoyed all our lives. I beg you to remember this, not only for my sake, but for yours. I happen, temporarily, to occupy this big White House. I am a living witness that any one of your children may look to come here as my father's child has. It is in order that each of you may have, through this free government which we have enjoyed, an open field and a fair chance for your industry, enterprize, and intelligence; that you may all have equal privileges in the race of life, with all its desirable human aspirations—it is for this that the struggle should be maintained, that we may not lose our birthrights, not only for one, but for two or three years, if necessary. The nation is worth fighting for, to secure such an inestimable jewel."

To divert Grant from Richmond, and Sherman from Atlanta, were now the chief aims of the Confederates. To say nothing of some mischievous and murderous raids from the British border, evidently devised only to embroil England with the United States, Missouri was for the third time invaded by General Price in October ; and though the Federal general in command, Rosecranz, whose right hand seemed to have forgot her cunning since Chattanooga, did little to check it, the Confederates ended by being routed, chiefly by Kansas militia, seconded by 5,000 Federal cavalry under Pleasanton, and withdrew, to return no more. Forrest, who had long succeeded in maintaining himself in Western Tennessee, was scouring with his cavalry to eastward, in order to destroy Sherman's communications. Acting in concert with him, Hood, with about 45,000 men, was operating (since about September 20) in Sherman's rear, destroying the railway line from Atlanta to Chattanooga, and attacking detached garrisons. All, no doubt, quite in accordance with the rules of war. But some men are able to make rules as well as to follow them.

To the same month of October belongs an important event in the civil history of the time—the adoption of an anti-slavery constitution by Maryland. Mr. Lincoln (October 10) wrote as follows on the subject before the vote:—

"It needs not to be a secret, and I presume it is no secret, that I wish success to this provision. . . . . I wish all men to be free. I wish the material prosperity of the already free, which I feel sure the extinction of slavery will bring. I wish to see in process of disappearing that only thing which ever could bring this nation to civil war."

Being serenaded by loyal Marylanders after the vote, Mr. Lincoln took the opportunity of replying to a calumnious charge then being made against him, that if he were not re-elected he would retain his functions in defiance of the law :—

" I am struggling to maintain the Government, not to overthrow it: I am struggling especially to prevent others from overthrowing it. I therefore say that, if I live, I shall remain President until the 4th of next March, and that whoever shall be constitutionally elected in November, shall be duly installed as President on the 4th of March, and in the interval I shall do my utmost that whoever is to hold the helm for the next voyage shall start with the best possible chance of saving the ship. This is due to the people, both on principle and under the Constitution. Their will, constitutionally expressed, is the ultimate law for all. If they should deliberately resolve to have immediate peace, even at the loss of their country and their liberties, I know not the power or the right to resist them. It is their own business, and they must do as they please with their own. I believe, however, they are still resolved to preserve their country and their liberties ; and in this, in office or out of it, I am resolved to stand by them. I may add, that in this purpose to save the country and its liberties, no classes of people seem so nearly unanimous as the soldiers in the field and the sailors afloat. Do they not have the hardest of it? Who should quail while they do not? God bless the soldiers and seamen, with all their brave commanders!"

I cannot stop over a letter written by the President in reply to an address from Tennessee, complaining of a test oath required by Governor Johnson (the present President) as a condition to the exercise of the franchise (October 22). Mr. Lincoln's conclusion was, that he "could have nothing to do with the matter," as, "by the constitution and laws, the President is charged with no duty in the conduct of the Presidential election in any state." A decision much cried out against at the time, but which was justified by the fact that the vote of Tennessee in his own favour was eventually disallowed by Congress.

And now came the fated 8th November with its Presidential election, which emphatically stamped the seal of national approval on Mr. Lincoln's policy, his term of office being renewed, not only by the votes of all the loyal states but three (Delaware, New Jersey, Kentucky), forming a majority sufficient to have carried his re-election had all the States in secession taken part in the election and voted against him, but by a larger popular majority (upwards of 365,000) than had ever been given in a contested Presidential election. Mr. Lincoln was serenaded, and replied as follows (10th November) :—

" It has long been a grave question whether any Government, not too strong for the liberties of its people, can be strong enough to maintain its own existence in great emergencies. On this point the present rebellion has brought our Republic to a severe test ; and the Presidential elections occurring in regular course during the rebellion, added not a little to the strain. If the loyal people united were put to the utmost of their strength by the rebellion, must they not fall when divided and partially paralysed by a political war among themselves? But the election was a necessity. We cannot have a free government without elections; and if a rebellion could force us to forego or postpone a national election, it might fairly claim to have already conquered us. . . . . But the rebellion continues, and now that the election is over, may not all having a common interest reunite in a common effort to save our common country? For my own part, I have striven and shall strive to avoid placing any obstruction in the way. So long as I have been here I have not willingly planted a thorn for any man's bosom. While I am duly sensible to the high compliment of a re-election, and duly grateful to Almighty God for having directed our countrymen to right conclusions, as I think, for their good, it adds nothing to my satisfaction that any other man may be disappointed by the result. May I ask those who have differed with me to join with me in this same spirit to those who have not? And now let me close by asking three hearty cheers for our brave soldiers and seamen, and their gallant and skilful commanders."

Those who may turn back to Mr. Lincoln's early speeches before and upon entering on the Presidential office, will feel the beautiful consistency with himself which the comparison exhibits throughout. Office has indeed now given him confidence in his own powers, yet without imparting the slightest tinge of vanity,* self-seeking, bitterness. His aim is still, as at the first, to lift men above the separating in-

---

* "I should be the most presumptuous blockhead upon this footstool," Mr. Lincoln said to Mr. Noah Brooks, one of his most intimate personal friends, just after his re-election, "if I for one day thought that I could discharge the duties which have come upon me since I came to this place, without the aid and enlightenment of One who is stronger and wiser than all others."

He said on another occasion :—" I am very sure that if I do not go away from here a wiser man I shall go away a better man, from having learned here what a very poor sort of a man I am."

fluence of party politics, into that sphere where they may unite their efforts for a common purpose. Moving in that higher sphere himself, his own pure spirit literally knows no political adversaries, but only fellow-countrymen, with whom he longs to work in fellowship. But it is now time to return to military operations.*

---

* The following private letter (Nov. 21) to a lady of Boston who had lost five sons in the war, and whose sixth was in hospital, seriously wounded, may here be inserted :—

"Dear Madam,—I have been shown in the files of the War Department a statement of the Adjutant-General of Massachusetts, that you are the mother of five sons who have died gloriously on the field of battle. I feel how weak and fruitless must be any words of mine which should attempt to beguile you from the grief of a loss so overwhelming. But I cannot refrain from tendering to you the consolation that may be found in the thanks of the Republic they died to save. I pray that our heavenly Father may assuage the anguish of your bereavement, and leave you only the cherished memory of the loved and lost, and the solemn pride that must be yours, to have laid so costly a sacrifice upon the altar of freedom.—Yours, very sincerely and respectfully,

"ABRAHAM LINCOLN."

We left Hood busily engaged in the orthodox task of destroying Sherman's communications with Chattanooga. After a period of seeming inaction, Sherman began following his enemy, not very closely pursuing him, but rather pushing him before him, and off the railway line to the westward. Then sending on General Thomas with all superfluous baggage and part of his artillery to Nashville, which he foresaw would serve as a bait to the Confederates, he rapidly doubled back, destroyed effectually that railway line which Hood had only destroyed imperfectly, destroyed Atlanta itself so as to prevent its serving any more as a stronghold or a rallying-point, and with 56,000 infantry, 5,000 cavalry under Kilpatrick, and about 58 12-pounders, began (November 16) the second of his great marches, this time from Atlanta towards the ocean, plunging into the heart of Georgia with ten days' rations, the troops marching in two bodies, on a line sometimes fifty miles wide, foraging and destroying the railways as they went.*　The Confederates had somehow got into their heads that he would kindly waste his time in marching towards Mobile (the forts guarding whose bay had been most gallantly carried by Admiral Farragut, and which was henceforth completely stopped up), and thereby place himself at the greatest possible distance

* For the details of Sherman's wonderful expedition, until Johnstone's final surrender, April 27th, 1865, see now "The Story of the Great March, by Brevet-Major George Ward Nichols, Aide-de-camp to General Sherman." (London : Sampson Low.) A controversy has lately arisen in our press as to the destruction exercised by Sherman's army, and in particular as to the burning of Columbia, the capital of South Carolina. Given the fact of war with its terrible necessities, the question, how much ravage and destruction it authorizes under any particular circumstances, is always one of the most difficult ones in ethics. I am bound to say, however, that from Major Nichols's own account, the discipline kept in Sherman's army appears to have fallen far short of what our Great Duke would have allowed : the rope and the lash would have been *his* mode of dealing with those "bummers," or private plunderers, whose existence as a class seems to have been at least winked at by the Federal General. On the other hand, it is certain that

from the operations in the North. So Beauregard, the celebrated Confederate engineer and tactician, lay in wait far to the westward at Corinth, whilst Hood and Forrest went floundering through the autumn mud of Tennessee towards Nashville, and nothing remained before Sherman to the eastward but one corps of

the Confederate ravages in Federal Tennessee, Kentucky, Missouri, exceeded and preceded at once those of Sherman. The burning of Chambersburg by express command of General Early, for non-payment of an enormous ransom, may be well set off against that of Columbia ; nor have the Federals to blush over any Fort Pillow massacre, or over the brutal maltreatment and starvation of the Confederate prisoners of war. But I must add that, at a time when an alleged rebellion in Jamaica, in which not half a hundred persons perished on the one side, and all but two or three of those in a single outbreak, has been, we are told, extinguished by the slaughter of 2,000 or more, on the other, and the burning of 4,000 houses by a single body of troops,—no resistance being ever offered, nor one single casualty being sustained, after the loss of life in the first conflict, massacre, and riots, it ill becomes Englishmen to be Pharisaically self-righteous over either Federal or Confederate barbarity.

Hood's army under Hardee, some Georgian militia, and some half-guerrilla cavalry under Wheeler.

For a month no certain news reached the North of his whereabouts, nor was the final development of any of these various movements known* when Mr. Lincoln addressed to Congress (6th Dec., 1864) his fourth—his last "annual message;" not of undue length, but too long to abstract. I may notice a kindly reference to the opening of official correspondence with Liberia, and a request (which was granted) "for authority to furnish to the Republic a gunboat at a moderate cost," to be reimbursed by instalments, for the protection of the State and the suppression of the slave-trade. Equally kindly was his reference to England and France, in speaking of the efforts of "disloyal emissaries" to "embroil our country in

---

* "We all know where he went in at," said Mr. Lincoln in reply to a serenade (evening of Dec. 16), speaking of Sherman, "but I can't tell where he will come out at."

foreign wars." He said, "The desire and determination of the maritime states to defeat that design are believed to be as sincere as, and cannot be more earnest than, our own." In view of late inroads from Canada, he had been obliged to give notice to England that, after the period of six months stipulated in existing arrangements, the United States must hold themselves at liberty to increase their naval armament on the lakes, while the condition of the border would necessarily come into consideration in connection with the Reciprocity Treaty, soon to be renewed or put an end to; but he desired to be understood that "the colonial authorities are not deemed to be intentionally unjust or unfriendly toward the United States." With an implied allusion to the charge of favouring the kidnapping of immigrants for military service, which had been loudly brought against the United States Government by Confederate sympathisers in Europe, he suggested amendments to a late Act for the encouragement of emigration, so as to secure to immigrants " a

o 2

free choice of avocations and places of settlement," since "the Government must in every
way make it manifest that it neither needs nor
designs to impose involuntary military service
upon those who come from other lands to cast
their lot in our country."

The financial portion of the message is per-
vaded by an anxious desire to secure the public
faith and credit by distributing the burthen of
the debt as widely as possible, and embraces
the novel proposal, framed by analogy with the
"Homestead" law of a few years previous, of
creating a kind of homesteads in the funds, *i.e.*,
limited amounts of the public securities to be
held free of taxes and exempt from seizure for
debt.   He briefly noticed the war, the general
advance of the army, the reorganisation of
Arkansas and Louisiana under free constitu-
tions, movements to the same effect in Missouri,
Kentucky, Tennessee; the free constitution
adopted in Maryland, "secure to liberty and
union for all the future;" the proposed amendment to the Constitution abolishing slavery,

which he recommended to be reconsidered and passed. He dwelt on the late election, on "the extraordinary calmness and good order" which marked it; on the fact that no candidate for office, high or low, had "ventured to seek votes on the avowal that he was for giving up the Union;" on the growth in population shown by the result of the polls; on the abundance of material resources possessed by the nation. He then passed to the means of re-establishing and maintaining the national authority. It did not seem to him that any attempt at negotiation with the insurgent leader could result in good, "since he would accept nothing short of the severance of the Union."

But what was true of the leader was not necessarily so of the followers. They could at any time "have peace simply by laying down their arms and submitting to the national authority." A year before, a general amnesty had been offered, subject to certain exceptions. Many had availed themselves of its provisions, and special pardons had been granted to individuals of excepted classes. But the time might come, and probably would, when public duty should demand that the door thus left open should be closed. And he concluded as follows :

" In presenting the abandonment of armed resistance to the national authority on the part of the insurgents as the only indispensable condition to ending the war on the part of the Government, I retract nothing heretofore said as to slavery. I repeat the declaration made a year ago, that while I remain in my present position I shall not attempt to retract or modify the emancipation proclamation ; nor shall I return to slavery any person who is free by the terms of that proclamation, or by any of the acts of Congress. *If the people should, by whatever means or process, make it an executive duty to re-enslave such persons, another, and not I, must be their instrument to perform it.* In stating a single condition of peace, I mean simply to say that the war will cease on the part of the Government whenever it shall have ceased on the part of those who began it."

Now came glorious news from Georgia and Tennessee. Sherman had at last debouched on the coast. His march had been little more than a military promenade, enlivened by a couple of skirmishes. Followed by droves of cattle and by thousands of fugitive slaves, his unthinned troops, "fat and well-liking" with the good cheer of Georgia, had completed that marvellous "retreat"—so called by some fool in *The Times*—which was to result in the reduction of well nigh all the Eastern sea-board of the Confederacy. After deceiving the enemy by a cavalry feint against Augusta, Sherman had presented himself before Fort Macalister, the only obstacle between him and Admiral Dahlgren's fleet, which was waiting for him off the coast, stormed it (Dec. 13), and, after a few days' siege, entered Savannah, which Hardee had evacuated (Dec. 21). Meanwhile, Thomas had justified Sherman's confidence, and his title to a chief command; had lured on Hood to destruction—staggered him by a first blow on the road to Nashville—then withdrawn

still further under the very walls of the city,
then turned on his enemy and crushed him
(Dec. 15). From henceforth the Confederate
army of the Tennessee practically ceased to
exist. The joy of these successes was indeed
partly marred by the failure of an attack by
sea and land upon Fort Fisher, one of the
defences of Wilmington, now the sole source of
foreign supply for Richmond (Dec. 25), from
which General Butler took upon himself the
responsibility of withdrawing, against the
opinion of Admiral Porter. The sequel to the
story may be disposed of at once. A new
attack was resolved upon ; a less eloquent, but
bolder, commander (General Terry) was placed
at the head of the troops, and whilst General
Butler was explaining to a committee of Congress that Fort Fisher could not have been
taken, news came that it was (15th Jan., 1865).
The other defences of Wilmington were blown
up by the Confederates or reduced, and the city
was entered (22nd Feb.) Sherman, meanwhile,
had commenced the third of his marches to the

northward. Penetrating to the very heart of
South Carolina, his occupation of its capital,
Columbia (17th Feb., 1865), caused Charleston,
which had so long baffled the utmost efforts of
the Federals, to fall at last without a blow (Feb.
18). He now turned eastward, to effect a
junction with Terry and Schofield, advancing
from Wilmington.

In the political sphere, the cause of freedom
was striding on. It deserves to be recorded as
an event in history, ·that on New Year's-day,
1865, the coloured people attended the Presidential reception at the White House.* But a

* Mr. Raymond thus relates the matter :—
" The Presidential reception on New Year's-day was
the occasion of a remarkable spectacle for Washington,
in the appearance of the coloured people at the White
House. They waited around the doors till the crowd of
white visitors diminished, when they made bold to enter
the hall. Some of them were richly dressed, while
others wore the garb of poverty ; but, alike intent on
seeing the man who had set their nation free, they
pressed forward, though with hesitation, into the presence of the President. Says an eye witness :—' For
nearly two hours Mr. Lincoln had been shaking the
hands of the " sovereigns " and had become excessively

more memorable one was the passage through Congress of the constitutional amendment, abolishing slavery. It had passed the Senate in the previous session, but had failed to obtain in the House of Representatives a majority of two-thirds, required for its validity. It was now carried in the latter body (Jan. 31) by 119 to 56, and now awaited only the necessary ratification by three-fourths of the States—almost all the most important of which, New York, Massachusetts, Pennsylvania, Illinois, &c., ratified it almost at once.* Mr. Lincoln, serenaded

weary, and his grasp became languid; but here his nerves rallied at the unwonted sight, and he welcomed this motley crowd with a heartiness that made them wild with exceeding joy. They laughed and wept, and wept and laughed—exclaiming through their blinding tears "God bless you! God bless Abraham Lincoln! God bless Massa Linkum!"'"

It is painful to have to add that President Johnson has not had the moral courage to follow in his predecessor's steps. On the 11th January, 1866, the coloured people were *not* admitted to the White House.

* On December 18th, 1865, the ratification of the amendment by the requisite twenty-seven out of the thirty-six States of the Union was proclaimed.

on the evening of the passing of the measure, spoke of the occasion as "one of congratulation to the country and to the whole world," and of the amendment itself as "a fitting, if not an indispensable, adjunct to the winding up of the great difficulty"—"a king's cure for all the evils."

A fresh negociation had meanwhile been opened with the Confederates, which was eventually carried on on their part through Mr. A. H. Stephens, their Vice-President, Senator Hunter of Virginia, and Judge Campbell. Mr. Davis had endeavoured to obtain recognition of the South by a side-wind, through a conference —"with a view to secure peace to *the two countries.*" (Jan. 12). Mr. Lincoln, on the other side, was willing to treat "with a view of securing peace to the people of *our common country*" (letter to Mr. Blair, Jan. 18). Substantially, his conditions were accepted, when Messrs. Stephens, Hunter, and Campbell agreed to "an informal conference with any person or persons that President Lincoln may appoint, on the basis of his letter to Francis P. Blair, of the 18th of January ultimo, or upon any other terms or conditions that he may hereafter propose, not inconsistent with the essential principles of self-government and popular rights upon which our institutions are founded" (Feb. 2). Mr. Lincoln and Mr. Seward met them personally on a steamer in Hampton Roads (Feb. 3). The bait was held out, if only the question of separation were postponed, and an armistice granted, of an alliance, offensive and defensive,—a war of conquest on Canada or Mexico. The Federal statesmen insisted on re-union, with an acceptance of all measures hitherto taken against slavery. The conference broke up, a failure*—

* From an account of the conference, said to have been prepared under the supervision of Mr. Stephens, and published in a Georgian paper (the *Augusta Chronicle*), it appears that Mr. Davis had made it a *sine quâ non* of regular negotiation that his own position as commander or president should be recognised. This Mr. Lincoln could not consent to. Mr. Hunter hereupon referred to the correspondence between King Charles the First and his Parliament as a precedent for

no doubt intended to be such by Mr. Davis—
and the failure was immediately made use of
by himself and his Secretary of State, Mr. Ben-
jamin, to provoke a revival of the war-fury in
the South, and to carry what both now saw to
be their last resource—the arming of the
negroes. But the time was long past when the
South could have outbid the North for the support of the slaves.

A final defeat by Sheridan of his old an-
tagonist, Early, nearly the whole of whose force
were taken prisoners, heralded brilliantly Mr.
Lincoln's resumption of the presidential office
(March 4, 1865). The text of his brief " Second
Inaugural " must be given in full :—

" Fellow-countrymen,—At this second ap-
pearing to take the oath of the Presidential

a negotiation between a constitutional ruler and rebels.
" Mr. Lincoln's face then wore that indescribable expression which generally preceded his hardest hits, and
he remarked :—' Upon questions of history I must
refer you to Mr. Seward, for he is posted in such things,
and I don't profess to be ; but my only distinct recol-
lection of the matter is, that Charles lost his head.' "

office, there is less occasion for an extended address than at first. Then a statement, somewhat in detail, of the course to be pursued, seemed very fitting and proper; now, at the expiration of four years, during which public declarations have constantly been called forth concerning every point and place of the great contest which still absorbs attention and engrosses the energies of the nation, little that is new could be presented.

" The progress of our arms, upon which all else chiefly depends, is as well known to the public as to myself. It is, I trust, reasonably satisfactory and encouraging to all. With a high hope for the future, no prediction in that regard is ventured.

" On the occasion corresponding to this four years ago, all thoughts were anxiously directed to an impending civil war. All dreaded it. All sought to avoid it. While the inaugural address was being delivered from this place, devoted altogether to saving the Union without war, the insurgent agents were in the city, seeking to destroy it without war—seeking to dissolve the Union and divide the effects by negotiating. Both parties deprecated war, but one of them would make war rather than let the nation survive, and the other would accept war rather than let it perish ; and war came.

" One-eighth of the whole population were coloured slaves, not distributed generally over the Union, but located in the Southern part. These slaves contributed a peculiar and powerful interest. All knew the interest would somehow cause war. To strengthen, perpetuate, and extend this interest was the object for which the insurgents would rend the Union by war, while the Government claimed no right to do more than restrict the territorial enlargement of it. Neither party expected the magnitude or duration which it has already attained ; neither anticipated that the cause of the conflict might cease even before the conflict itself should cease. Each looked for an easier triumph, and a result less fundamental and astonishing. Both read the same Bible and pray to the same God.

Each invokes His aid against the other. It may
seem strange that any man should dare to ask
a just God's assistance in wringing bread from
the sweat of other men's faces ; but let us judge
not, that we be not judged. The prayer of both
could not be answered ; that of neither has been
answered fully ; for the Almighty has His own
purposes. 'Woe unto the world because of
offences, for it must needs be that offences come ;
but woe to that man by whom the offence
cometh !' If we shall suppose American
slavery one of those offences which in the
Providence of God must needs come, but
which, having continued through His appointed
time, He now wills to remove, and that He
gives to both North and South this terrible war,
as was due to those by whom the offence came,
shall we discern that there is any departure
from those divine attributes which believers in
the living God always ascribe to Him ? Fondly
do we hope, fervently do we pray, that this
mighty scourge of war may speedily pass away ;
yet if it is God's will that it continue until the

wealth piled by bondsmen by 250 years' unrequited toil shall be sunk, and until every drop of blood drawn with the lash shall be paid by another drawn with the sword, as was said 3,000 years ago, so still it must be said, that the judgments of the Lord are true and righteous altogether.

"With malice towards none, with charity for all, with firmness in the right, as God gives us to see the right, let us strive on to finish the work we are in, to bind up the nation's wounds, to care for who shall have borne the battle, and for his widow and orphans ; to do all which may achieve and cherish a just and a lasting peace among ourselves and with all nations."

Loftier, weightier words were surely never spoken by any ruler. In this rail-splitter, the exercise of the highest power has only brought out a deeper reverence for that just Being who is the source of all power, a more humble submission to His will, a more profound faith in His righteousness. Oh, for a few more such believers in the living God!

P

Side by side with this message may be placed, by way of contrast, part of a speech of March 17, on the occasion of the presentation of a captured flag, in reference to the attempt then being made by the Confederates to enlist the coloured men :—

"I have in my lifetime heard many arguments why the negroes ought to be slaves; but if they fight for those who would keep them in slavery, it will be a better argument than any I have yet heard. . . . While I have often said that all men ought to be free, yet would I allow those coloured persons to be slaves who want to be, and, next to them, those white people who argue in favour of making other people slaves. . . . I will say one thing in regard to the negro being employed to fight for them. I do know he cannot fight and stay at home and make bread too. And as one is about as important as the other to them, I don't care which they do; I am rather in favour of having them try them as soldiers. . . . We must now see the bottom of the enemy's resources. They will stand out as long as they can; and if the negro will fight for them they must allow him to fight. I am glad to see the end so near at hand."

The end is indeed near at hand. Sherman has reached Fayetteville (11th March), only within 200 miles from Grant, Hardee evacuating it on his approach, and is marching upon Goldsborough. His old antagonist, Johnstone, has been restored to command, and fronts him once more; he strikes one somewhat vigorous blow on Sherman's left wing at Bentonville (18th March), but his strength is well nigh spent. Goldsborough is occupied after a little more fighting (21st—22nd March). Sherman is within 140 miles of Grant. All now turns upon Lee. The very day after President Lincoln, worn to death by the obsession of office-seekers, has sought a refuge under the enemy's cannon, in a visit to the army of the Potomac (which he was not to leave henceforth till after the taking of Richmond, and of which the final achievements were to be communicated to the people by telegrams under their President's own hand), a night attack on Grant's right is momentarily successful (25th March) ; but the Confederates have to withdraw at daybreak, leaving 1200 men behind. Meanwhile, the Confederate forces in the Shenandoah Valley being annihilated, Sheridan has come round to City Point on the James with his troops, victors in so many fights (28th March). Sent to the extreme right of Lee's line, to cut off the last line of communication between Richmond and the South, he wins his wonderful victory of Five Forks, chiefly with dismounted cavalry (1st April), thus severing Lee from Johnstone. The main body of Grant's army now attacks the Confederate lines, and forces them ; Petersburg is evacuated, then Richmond (3rd April).* Lee tries to escape by the South-West,

---

* The day after the evacuation of Richmond, Mr. Lincoln entered the city—in what fashion, I shall borrow Dr. Storr's eloquent pen to describe :—

" After four years of incessant, bloody, desperate struggle, he entered Richmond, with characteristic unostentation—not at the head of marshalled armies, with banners advanced and trumpets sounding, but as a

but is pursued by Sheridan, who, on the 6th April, strikes one of his retreating columns, and takes 6,000 prisoners, including six generals. Grant immediately opens negociations for surrender with his worthy, but unsuccessful antagonist; and, after a correspondence equally honourable to both parties, the Confederate army of Northern Virginia is surrendered by its veteran commander (9th April).* Two days

private gentleman, on foot, with an officer on one side, holding the hand of his boy on the other. An aged negro met him in the street, and said, with the tears streaming down his face, as he bowed low his uncovered head,—' God bress you, Massa Lincoln !' The President paused, raised his hat on the instant, and with a hearty 'I thank you, sir,' acknowledged with a bow the greeting. Instinctively, he recognised the poorest as his peer, and the black man as his brother." (Oration, pp. 19-20).

An eye-witness of the scene, who, however, says that the President " bowed in silence," adds : " A woman in an adjoining house beheld it, and turned from the scene in unspeakable disgust." (Raymond, pp. 682-3).

* " On the day of the receipt of the capitulation of Lee, the cabinet meeting was held an hour earlier than usual. Neither the President nor any member was able, later,—whilst Sherman's army, "in the grandest of spirits," was marching upon Raleigh, the capital of North Carolina—Abraham Lincoln made his last speech (April 11th, 1865) :—

" We meet this evening, not in sorrow, but in gladness of heart. The evacuation of Petersburgh and Richmond, and surrender of the principal insurgent army, gives hopes of a righteous peace, whose joyous expression cannot be restrained. In the midst of this, however, He from whom all blessings flow must not be forgotten. A call for a national thanksgiving is being prepared, and will be duly promulgated. Nor must those whose harder part gives us the cause of rejoicing be overlooked ; their honours must not be parcelled out with others. I myself was near the front, and had the high pleasure of transmitting much of the good news

or a time, to give utterance to his feelings. At the suggestion of Mr. Lincoln, all dropped on their knees, and offered, in silence and in tears, their humble and heartfelt acknowledgments to the Almighty for the triumph He had granted to the national cause." (Raymond, p. 735). Can history afford a nobler picture ?

to you; but no part of the honour for the plan
or execution is mine. To General Grant, his
skilful officers, and brave men, it all belongs.
The gallant navy stood ready, but was not in
reach to take active part. By these recent
successes, the re-inauguration of the national
authority, the reconstruction of which has had
a large share of thought from the first, is pressed
most strongly upon our attention. It is fraught
with great difficulty. Unlike a case of war between independent nations, there is no authorized
organ for us to treat with, no one man has authority to give up the rebellion for any other man.
We simply must begin with and mould from
disorganised and discordant elements. Nor is
it a small additional embarrassment that we,
the loyal people, differ among ourselves as to the
mode, manner, and measure of reconstruction."

And now, to the astonishment of many no
doubt, and probably to the disgust of some of
his hearers, he goes into the question of the
Louisiana State Government, and never gets out
of it during the rest of the speech. As a

general rule, he abstains from reading the reports of attacks upon himself. But he knows that he has been much censured for some supposed agency in getting up and seeking to sustain the new State Government of Louisiana, constructed in accordance with the plan annexed to his annual message of 1863. Others regret that his mind has not seemed " definitely fixed on the question whether the Seceded States, so called, are in the Union or not." That question he believes to be "bad as a basis of controversy, and good for nothing at all." If all will only " join in doing the acts necessary to restore the proper practical relations" between these States and the Union, each " may then for ever after innocently indulge his own opinion, whether in doing the acts he brought the States from without into the Union, or only gave them proper assistance, they never having been out of it."

It would no doubt be more satisfactory if the constituency on which the Louisiana Government rests were 50,000, 30,000, 20,000, rather than 12,000. " It is also unsatisfactory to some that the elective franchise is not given to the coloured race. I would myself prefer that it were now conferred on the very intelligent, and on those who serve our cause as soldiers." Still the fact remains, that some 12,000 voters in the heretofore slave State of Louisiana have " adopted a free state constitution, giving the benefit of the public schools equally to white and black, and empowering the Legislature to confer the elective franchise upon the coloured man "; and this same Legislature " has already voted to ratify the constitutional amendment recently passed by Congress abolishing slavery throughout the nation."

" Concede that the new Government of Louisiana is only to what it should be as the egg is to the fowl, we shall sooner have the fowl by hatching the egg than by smashing it. . . . No exclusive and inflexible plan can safely be prescribed as to details and collaterals. . . . Important principles may, and must be, inflexible. In the present situation, as the phrase goes, it may be my duty to make some new

announcement to the people of the South.   I
am considering, and shall not fail to act when
satisfied that action will be proper."

When we consider that only three days later
(April 14th) the speaker met his tragic death-
stroke, we may be tempted to wish that some
grander, larger words had fallen from his lips
on such an occasion.   And yet the speech has a
quiet majesty of its own.   Surely no man ever,
more perfectly realized those words of St. Paul,
"Forgetting those things which are behind,
and reaching forth unto those things which are
before."   Behind is a four years' struggle for
the very life of the nation, gigantic, world-
famous; behind are Sherman's strides of
triumph, and Grant's patient strategy, and
Sheridan's meteor-like successes, and the fall of
the rival capital, and the surrender of a great
general and of a long-victorious army; yet all
is forgotten in a moment by him who more than
any other has the right to rest upon present
blessings, since he has borne the whole burthen
of past anxieties and sorrows, whilst he reaches

forth to the things before,—to the reconstitu-
tion of the South on its new basis of freedom,
and in particular to this Louisiana State Constitution.   There lies his present duty, and how
to fulfil that duty is now all his care.   That he
judged rightly as to the importance of the question of negro suffrage it is impossible to deny.
I am not indeed prepared to say that he saw his
way to the right solution of it.   But what I
do say is, that no one could have uttered such
a speech at such a moment, but one in whose
soul duty was a fixed, dominant, nay, all-absorb-
ing principle; one who, simply and without
effort, was fulfilling the wise man's precept:
" Whatsoever thine hand findeth to do, do it
with thy might."*

The 14th of April came.   But for what was

* The perfect self-consistency of Mr. Lincoln's moral
character may be illustrated by a comparison of this
speech with the closing passage of one delivered by him
before his first nomination, at the Cooper Institute, New
York, on Feb. 27, 1860 :—" Let us have faith that right
makes might, and in that faith let us to the end dare to
do our duty as we understand it."   Words which might
have served as a motto for his whole life.

to follow at Washington, it might have been marked in the country's history only by Sherman's occupation of a third conquered State capital, Raleigh, North Carolina; and by the raising of the United States flag once more upon Fort Sumter, on the anniversary of its surrender in 1862 by the same officer who had then defended it. After breakfasting with his son, Captain Robert Lincoln, who had witnessed Lee's surrender, the President received several public men, amongst others, Speaker Colfax, who was about to proceed overland to the Pacific coast. His words to Mr. Colfax have been recorded :—

"Mr. Colfax, I want you to take a message from me to the miners whom you visit. I have very large ideas of the mineral wealth of our nation. I believe it practically inexhaustible, ... and its development has scarcely commenced. During the war, when we were adding a couple of millions of dollars every day to our national debt, I did not care about encouraging the increase in the volume of our precious metals. We had the country to save first. But now that the rebellion is overthrown, and we know pretty nearly the amount of our national debt, the more gold and silver we receive, we make the payment of that debt so much the easier. Now I am going to encourage that in every possible way. We shall have hundreds of thousands of disbanded soldiers, and many have feared that their return home in such numbers might paralyse industry, by furnishing suddenly a greater supply of labour than there will be demand for. I am going to try to attract them to the hidden wealth of our mountain ranges, where there is room enough for all. Immigration, which even the war has not stopped, will land upon our shores hundreds of thousands more per year from over-crowded Europe. I intend to point them to the gold and silver that wait for them in the West. Tell the miners from me that I shall promote their interests to the utmost of my ability; because their prosperity is the prosperity of the nation; and we shall prove, in a very few years, that we are indeed the treasury of the world."

Full of these golden hopes,—thus already

intent on the promotion of those arts of peace,
through which he hoped to lessen the burthen
of the nation's obligations,—he went forth to
that last Cabinet Council, of which the touching
record remains, that "he spoke very kindly of
Lee and others of the Confederacy." His
mood, Mrs. Lincoln has lately stated, had
become far more cheerful; even when going
down the Potomac to the army he had been
"almost boyish in his mirth." But on that
terrible Friday—

"His manner was even playful. At three
o'clock he drove out with me in the open car-
riage. In starting, I asked him if any one
should accompany us? He immediately replied,
'No, I prefer to ride by ourselves to-day.'
During the drive he was so gay, that I said to
him laughingly, 'Dear husband, you almost
startle me by your great cheerfulness.' He
replied, 'And well I may feel so, Mary, for I
consider this day the war has come to a close';
and then added, 'We must both be more cheerful in the future. Between the war and the

loss of our darling Willie,* we have been very miserable.' "

He still found time that afternoon to pen one public document, of special value to us Englishmen, the draft of a reply to Sir F. Bruce, on his forthcoming first presentation as British Minister, outlined indeed by Mr. Seward, but which was only to be read by his successor (20th April). No notice of his state papers and speeches can be sufficient which does not include this voice from the grave—this last solemn token of Abraham Lincoln's friendly feeling towards our country and our sovereign :—

" Sir Frederick Bruce —Sir : the cordial and

* The loss of this favourite son was reckoned by Mr. Lincoln himself as a turning-point in his spiritual history. " That blow," he said on one occasion, " overwhelmed me. It showed me my weakness, as I had never felt it before."

In the spring of 1862, being at Fortress Monroe, he once called to his aide-de-camp, Colonel Cannon, who was in the adjoining room, " You have been writing long enough, Colonel, come in here ; I want to read you a passage in ' Hamlet.' " He read the discussion on ambition between Hamlet and his courtiers, and the soliloquy in which conscience debates of a future state.

friendly sentiments which you have expressed on the part of Her Britannic Majesty gave me great pleasure. Great Britain and the United States, by the extended and varied forms of commerce between them, the contiguity of positions of their possessions, and the similarity of their language and laws, are drawn into contrast and intimate intercourse at the same time. They are from the same causes exposed to frequent occasions of misunderstanding, only to be averted by mutual forbearance. So eagerly are the people of the two countries engaged

This was followed by passages from "Macbeth." Then opening to "King John," he read from the third act the passage in which Constance bewails her imprisoned lost boy. Then closing the book, and recalling the words :—
"And, father Cardinal, I have heard you say
  That we shall see and know our friends in heaven:
  If that be true, I shall see my boy again."
Mr. Lincoln said, "Colonel, did you ever dream of a lost friend, and feel that you were holding sweet communion with that friend, and yet have a sad consciousness that it was not a reality? Just so I dream of my boy Willie." Overcome with emotion, he dropped his head on the table, and sobbed aloud. (From Mr. Carpenter's "Anecdotes," *passim.*)

throughout almost the whole world in the pursuit
of similar commercial enterprises, accompanied
by natural rivalries and jealousies, that at first
sight it would almost seem that the two governments must be enemies, or at best cold and
calculating friends. So devoted are the two
nations throughout all their domain, and even
in their most remote territorial and colonial
possessions, to the principles of civil rights and
constitutional liberty, that on the other hand
the superficial observer might erroneously count
upon a continued consent of action and sympathy, amounting to an alliance between them.
Each is charged with the development of the
progress and liberty of a considerable portion of
the human race. Each in its sphere is subject
to difficulties and trials not participated in by
the other. *The interests of civilization and
humanity require that the two should be friends.*
I have always known, and accepted it as a fact,
honourable to both countries, that the Queen of
England is a sincere and honest well-wisher of
the United States, and have been equally frank
and explicit in the opinion that the friendship

of the United States towards Great Britain is enjoined by all the considerations of interest and of sentiment affecting the character of both. You will therefore be accepted as a Minister friendly and well-disposed to the maintenance of peace and the honour of both countries. You will find myself and all my associates acting in accordance with the same enlightened policy and consistent sentiments; and so I am sure that it will not occur in your case, that either yourself or this Government will ever have cause to regret that such an important relationship existed at such a crisis."

And so, at a little after eight p.m., he went forth to meet his martyr's doom.*

* The details of the dread tragedy at Ford's Theatre should still be fresh in our minds. The following account, however, of what took place, compressed from Mr. Raymond's (which must be considered as authoritative), may not here be superfluous :—

The play was "Our American Cousin." In a double box, with a vestibule behind, and with a front of about ten feet looking upon the stage, from which hung the United States' flag, sate the President in a rocking chair, Mrs. Lincoln on his right; two other persons,

In dealing with President Lincoln's speeches
and writings, I have avoided all but incidental

Miss Harris and Major Rathbone, her step-brother,
being in the box. The box-door was directly behind
him, and remained open during the night ; an attendant
sate a few feet from the outer door of the vestibule. At
a quarter-past ten, the actor, John Wilkes Booth, passing along the passage behind the spectators, showed a
card to the attendant, and after standing for two or
three minutes, looking down on the stage, entered the
vestibule of the President's box, closed the door behind
him, fastened it, and then entering the door of the box
itself, as the President was leaning forward, shot him
with a small pistol through the back of the head. Mr.
Lincoln's head fell slightly forward, and his eyes closed,
but his attitude remained unchanged. Hearing the
report, Major Rathbone sprang forward and seized
Booth, who, however, wrested himself from his grasp,
wounding him severely with a long double-edged dagger,
which he carried in his left hand, then rushed to the
front, shouting " *Sic semper tyrannis*," and leaped over
upon the stage ; but his spur caught in the " Stars and
Stripes," and he fell, breaking his leg. He sprang, however, to his feet, brandishing his dagger, and shouting
again, " The South is avenged," succeeded in making his
escape to the outer door of the theatre, where he mounted
a horse, which was waiting for him. Embarrassed at

Q 2

notice of those "good stories" and "jokes," of
which so many have been fathered on him that
were not his.   All the more authentic of these
are no doubt included in Mr. Carpenter's
interesting "Anecdotes and Reminiscences" on
which I have frequently drawn, and which I
heartily commend to my readers.   It has been
said of Mr. Lincoln, by one of the most eloquent

once and tracked by his broken leg, he was, as is well
known, eventually shot down like a wild beast in its
lair (26th April), in a barn, on the south of the Rappahannock ; so that, by a mysterious justice, the national
flag may be said to have avenged its great standard-
bearer.

Mr. Lincoln never recovered speech or consciousness.
The ball had entered three inches behind the left ear,
traversing obliquely the brain, and lodging just behind
the right eye.   At twenty-two minutes past seven a.m.
of the 15th he expired.   "There was no convulsive
action, no rattling in the throat, no appearance of suffering of any kind, none of the symptoms which ordinarily
attend dissolution, and add to its terrors."   The words
of Petrarch might have been applied to him,—he
"seemed to rest like one a-weary," ,

Parea posar come persona stanca.

Weary no doubt of earth, but fresh for heaven.

of living men :* "His very colloquialisms were mighty 'for his service. 'We must keep still pegging away,' he said, in the gloomiest part of the war ; and every plain man saw his duty, and was nerved to perform it. 'One war at a time,'—all the orators could not answer it ; a unanimous press could not have overborne the impression it made. 'The United States Government must not undertake to run the churches:'— the *dictum* is worth a half-dozen duodecimos on the complex relations of Church and State. 'You needn't cross a bridge until you have got to it :'—if men's minds were not relieved of their fears concerning the effect of a general emancipation, they were at least widely persuaded to postpone these, by the fitting advice." As respects his jokes, properly so called, one who had close opportunities of observation, said, in reply to a question how the President endured the cares and labours that were upon him, " Nothing keeps him up but his habit of joking.

* Dr. Storrs, in his before referred to " Oration commemorative of President Abraham Lincoln."

This affords him momentary, but complete relaxation, and is, I believe, the safety valve of his mind." Yet "nothing about Mr. Lincoln," we are told, "has led to more complete misconception than this habit of joking. It has been, by those who did not know him, attributed to levity. Nothing was further from the truth. His jokes and stories were, in fact, his medium of illustration, and were always wonderfully to the point."*

There remains for me only to ask, whether the speeches and papers I have referred to, do not show us one who stands forth, self-pourtrayed in them to all time, among the purest and noblest of rulers whom this earth has ever known?

---

* Mr. Lincoln himself said, on one occasion, during the dark days of 1862, Mr. Carpenter tells us, "Were it not for this occasional *vent*, I should die." And of this "coarse buffoon," as the hounds of the press were wont to call him, the artist has written, "It has been the business of my life to study the human face, and I have said repeatedly to friends that Mr. Lincoln had the saddest face I ever attempted to paint."

THE MARTYRED PRESIDENT.

(From *Good Words*, June 1, 1865.*)

WITHIN the last few weeks a common sorrow
has spread throughout our land, such as has never
befallen it since the day when England's Prince
was stricken down in the fulness of his manhood.
And yet it is for no prince, noble, statesman,
patriot, whom we have been accustomed to see
among us, to look up to, or to follow. He
never trod the soil of our islands; not one in
many thousands among us ever saw his face.
An ocean separated us from him; he ruled over
another State. And yet, at such an hour as
this, we feel that ABRAHAM LINCOLN was indeed

* I have let these pages stand as first published, with
the exception of a few words (either restored from the
original draft, or inserted to correct a misapprehension),
and of the note at the end.

bone of our bone and flesh of our flesh—that
the great race which reads the Bible in the same
mother-tongue on both sides of the Atlantic,
whatever differences of polity may separate its
various fractions, is yet but one people. Strange
workings of a Hand mightier than man's! The
pistol of an assassin—born, it would seem, of an
English father on American soil—has done more
to bring this country and America together
than all the years which have elapsed since a
monarch's obstinacy tore them asunder. O!
how blessedly different from those times of
bitter fratricidal strife are these, when a widowed
English Queen, anticipating the almost universal instinct of her people, could of her own
accord address at once, in her own hand, to that
other widow across the Atlantic, the expression
of her deep sympathy for the murder of the
chief magistrate of the United States!

It were waste of time here to express horror
at a crime which, taking it with all its circumstances, stands unexampled in political history.
The wrath of man worketh not the righteousness

of God. Let us be content with awe to remember those words: " Vengeance is mine,
saith the Lord; I will repay." Yea, He will
repay! The blood of the innocent was never
shed before His eyes in vain. A deed as hideous
as any, since that Carpenter who was the Son of
God hung between heaven and earth on the slave's
cross, has been perpetrated on his lowly follower,
whom the Pharisees of this world mocked as a
" rail-splitter," a "bargee," a "village attorney."
He who is higher than the highest regardeth.
The Judge of all the earth shall do right.

But God's vengeance is not as man's vengeance. His justice is shown by sparing the
many guilty for the sake of the few righteous.
His doom for sin was the sending of a Saviour.
The revenge of martyrdom is never fulfilled but
by the conversion of the world, which slew the
martyrs, to the truths for which they bore witness.
ABRAHAM LINCOLN, Freedom's last and greatest
martyr, can only be avenged by the conversion
to freedom of the slave-world. Already we
have heard of the grief of Lee, of the tears of

Ewell. Who can tell in how many bosoms horror
of the crime will not ripen into abhorrence of
the evil root from which it sprang? Who can
tell how many gallant but hitherto misguided
Southerners it will not rally to the 'cause of
that Union which their fathers loved, worked
for, fought for? By the thrill of sympathy
which it has awakened amongst ourselves, may
we not judge how much mightier should be that
which it will awaken in men not only speaking
the same language, but long united as one
nation by a thousand ties of neighbourhood,
interest, kinship, fellow-help and fellow-work?
Take that simple record of ABRAHAM LINCOLN'S
last-recorded hour of statesmanship: " He
spoke very kindly of Lee." Oh, what a revenge
was there already by anticipation for Booth's
pistol-shot, over all Secessionists who bore yet
a human heart within their bosom! And let
us remember that it is not only an American
that has fallen, but a Southerner born, a child
of the Slave-State of Kentucky, and one who in
youth had largely mingled with the men of the

South, and worked for his bread among them; and that this it is which gave such weight to that testimony of his against slavery, which he has at last sealed with his blood. Let us rest assured, that to many a truly gentle and chivalrous heart at the South that blood will henceforth appeal in tones no longer to be resisted. Most remarkable is it indeed that the great witnesses for Union alike and for Freedom have in America almost always been Southern men, by birth or domicile. Jefferson the Virginian gives for first utterance to American nationality that Declaration of Independence which proclaims the natural freedom and equality of all mankind; Washington, and the other great Virginian Presidents who follow him, establish the Union; Jackson the South Carolinian, with his Secretary of State, Livingstone of Louisiana, arrests for awhile its destruction, when threatened by the hotheaded "Nullificationists" of the South. And now, in the fulness of the times, the Kentuckian LINCOLN spends his life in the earnest endeavour to restore the Union on the ground of universal freedom, leaving his high office and the fulfilment of his task to another Southerner, the North Carolinian Andrew Johnson. Will not the South understand at last that Secession is treason against its own purest glories, against the fair fame of its greatest men?

We indeed must see that the cause of that Slave-Power, which declared that slavery was to be the corner-stone of its Government, has now melted away for ever in the blood of its latest · victims. Acquit, as we most willingly should, the leaders of Secession of all complicity in the foul deed, yet it is the accursed spirit of slavery which spoke in the deed, in the words of the assassin. " Thus be it always with tyrants!" cried the frantic ruffian, as he escaped across the stage, after having shot an unarmed man through the back of the head, by his wife's side, and in the midst of his countrymen. An utterance which would be ludicrous, if it were not ghastly,—if it did not indicate that utter per-version of man's spirit which the mere tolerance of slavery engenders, making him call evil good and good evil, and to mistake for a tyrant the man whose proud privilege throughout all time shall be, that he proclaimed freedom to four millions of his fellow-men. What superstructure the corner-stone of slavery may bear, the whole world should see henceforth.

The great American people, could we have understood the facts of a struggle, long shamefully misrepresented by a too large portion of our press, has been from the beginning, is doubly henceforth, entitled to our fullest sympathies, whilst engaged in its present gigantic task of self-purification and self-reform. That God's blessing has rested upon it throughout that struggle,—in the arts of peace and in the arts of war,—in the reverses which it has known how to bear, and in the triumphs which it has known how to wait for, and when achieved, how to use,—in the valour of its generals, in the wisdom and gentleness of its rulers,—above all, in the steadfast self-devotion of its masses, we cannot doubt. The clash of warfare may be well-nigh over, but a vast work yet remains to be done.   Let us hope and pray that it may be worthily fulfilled, and that upon a basis of large forgiveness for the errors of the past, but at the same time of equal rights and equal duties for all classes of citizens of whatever colour, a renewed Union may be built up, free from many of the political imperfections of the old, more truly worthy of the admiration of the world ; and that the name of LINCOLN may inaugurate a series of rulers, who shall endear themselves even more to their countrymen than Washington and his great contemporaries did to their forefathers.

To the martyred President, such a Union will be the only true earthly monument ; to his bereaved family, it will be the highest earthly consolation.   *He* stands far above all puny pity of ours.   That Lord whom he acknowledged in all his acts, and in none more signally than in that second Inaugural Message of his,—one of the noblest state-papers, because one of the lowliest, that ever dropped from the pen of an earthly ruler,—has called him to Himself.   Shall we rebel, and say that it was too soon ? It is written : " When the fruit is brought forth, IMMEDIATELY He putteth in the sickle, because the harvest is come." Immediately,—whether that sickle take the shape of disease, or old age, or accident, or the assassin's pistol-shot ; immediately,—for the Lord of the harvest knows without fail when the fruit is brought forth.* Let us rest assured that for that brave and gentle spirit the suddenness of death had no terrors, and that to the voice of Him who is saying for ever, " Surely I come quickly," his only answer would be, " Even so, come, Lord Jesus."

* We are now able to see that death sealed more triumphantly the completeness of Abraham Lincoln's work, than any lengthening of his life could have done ; since Booth's crime (perhaps the most futile as respects its purpose that ever was committed), availed not to disarrange for a single day the working of the Federal institutions,—did not shake the discipline of a corporal's guard, nor delay the surrender of one Confederate. Abraham Lincoln had indeed fulfilled to the uttermost that " most solemn" oath of his (see *ante*, p. 39), to " preserve, protect, and defend " the Government of his country.